新制多益
閱讀搶分寶典

1駅1題! TOEIC L&R TEST 読解特急

多益兩大滿分天王

神崎正哉✕TEX 加藤

Daniel Warriner _著

蕭志億_審訂

QR Code

新制多益考試介紹&改制重點

TOEIC L & R TEST 考試介紹

TOEIC 聽力與閱讀測驗分成七大部分，**Part 1-4 為聽力部分**，共 100 題，作答時間 45 分鐘。**Part 5-7 為閱讀部分**，共 100 題，作答時間 75 分鐘。聽力部分配分 495 分，閱讀配分 495 分，共 990 分。

多益新舊制考試比較

	Part	內容	舊制題數	新制題數	備註
聽力	1	照片敘述	10	6	
	2	應答問題	30	25	
	3	簡短對話	30	39	新增〈3 人對話〉、〈5 句以上對話〉、〈理解意圖〉
	4	簡短獨白	30	30	新增〈理解圖表〉、〈理解意圖〉
閱讀	5	句子填空	40	30	
	6	段落填空	12	16	新增〈選出符合上下文的句子〉
	7	單篇閱讀	28	29	新增〈線上聊天閱讀〉、〈理解意圖〉、〈插入句子〉、〈3 篇閱讀〉
		雙篇閱讀	20	10	
		3 篇閱讀	0	15	

臺灣自 2018 年 3 月起，實施 New TOEIC 新制多益，新制總題數與考試時間雖然不變，但各部分的題型與題數皆有調整，簡單的題型如 Part 1-2、Part 5 題數減少，並新增新題型，如〈理解圖表問題〉、〈文章脈絡問題〉、〈3 篇閱讀〉等，在閱讀理解上難度增加。

Contents 目錄

Part 7 高分關鍵：閱讀理解＋速度＋掌握題型

日本多益兩大天王
神崎正哉、TEX 加藤

1. 提升閱讀理解力

TOEIC 測驗共 200 題，其中 Part 7 的閱讀理解題就有 54 題，佔了整體考試四分之一，是相當大的篇幅。因此，如果你能在 Part 7 閱讀理解拿下高分，就能大大提升整體多益分數。想精進閱讀能力沒有別的途徑，養成平時大量閱讀英文文章的習慣就對了。平時進行英文閱讀，可以提升大腦處理英文的速度，能讓你更快理解英文，也能提升聽力與文法題的解題速度。

2. 掌握時間分配

有些考生總是無法在 Part 7 拿分，是因為他們不習慣看這種彙整了各種資訊的長篇英文文章。Part 7 需要讀者閱讀好幾篇文章，如果是不習慣閱讀的人，光看到這一長篇的英文就嚇傻了。

此外，Part 7 都是大量的英文文章，需要較長的作答時間。因此，時間管理尤為關鍵。如果你能控制在 60 秒回答完一題，在時間結束前寫完所有題目，你就相當於掌握 Part 7 分數。

3. 掌握題型

要提升答題速度，就要掌握 Part 7 的題型與解題技巧。TOEIC 的題目無論是哪個大題都有固定的題型，熟悉題型的話就能迅速、正確解決題目。

本書使用說明

☑ **暖身篇**：熟悉閱讀出題題型
☑ **Part 1**：先提升閱讀速度
☑ **Part 2**：再提高作答正確性

1. 務必細讀本書所有的文章與題目。

實際應考時，Part 7 的題目不必讀完全部文章也能作答，但練習本書題目時，請先讀完整篇文章與每題題目。不先練習閱讀的話，是無法看懂題目的，千萬不要看問題再回去跳看文章，記得先仔細閱讀本文來理解內容。然後，請盡量加快解題速度。

2. 寫完所有題目之後一定要對答案。

如果文章或題目中出現不懂的詞句，要查解釋並記起來。本書每篇文章後都有標出重要單字，請善加活用。

3. 本書所有文章皆有音檔 ◎。

閱讀後可聽音檔確認發音，加強聽力。閱讀速度較慢的人，不妨試試搭配音檔閱讀，念到哪就看到哪，對於提升閱讀速度相當有效，務必試看看。

音檔
使用説明

STEP **1**

掃描此 QR Code

STEP **2**

立即註冊

- 帳號　限3-21碼小寫英文數字
- 信箱
- 密碼　限8-24碼小寫英文數字
　　　　再次輸入密碼

完成

社群帳號註冊

f 使用Facebook註冊

Google　使用Gooel註冊

已經註冊？　　**登入**

□ 註冊即同意 隱私權及 安全政策

可選「快速註冊」或「登入」EZCourse

STEP **3**

請回答以下問題完成訂閱

一、請問本書第65頁，紅色框線中的英文＿＿＿是什麼？

答案　請注意大小寫

二、請問本書第33頁，紅色框線中的英文＿＿＿是什麼？

答案　請注意大小寫

送出

回答問題之後按「送出」，通過認證

答案就在書中
（填寫答案時需注意空格與大小寫）。

STEP **4**

按下訂閱

該書右側會顯示「已訂閱」，
表示已成功訂閱，
即可點選播放本書音檔。

STEP **5**

帳號設定

< 個人檔案 | 會員資料 >

EZ Course+　EZCourse

我的訂閱記錄

點選個人訂閱記錄

查看「我的訂閱記錄」
會顯示已訂閱本書，
點選封面即可線上聆聽音檔。

新制多益 Part 7
十大出題類型

1. 詢問細節題

> 基本題，從文中找出與題目有關的資訊。

When does Michelle Carter wish to visit Brick First Real Estate?

(A) March 16
(B) March 17
(C) March 25
(D) March 26

······ 完整題目請見 P. 021

解題技巧

- 先找出題目關鍵字，在文章中搜尋相關資訊，就能找出答案。如例題關鍵字為：人名 Michelle Carter、公司名 Brick First Real Estate 與 When。
- 看清楚題目問的是何種資訊，如例題詢問的是 When「何時」，透過掌握題目的 wh 疑問詞，也可在文中快速搜尋到想要的資訊。

2. 文章主旨題

> **What is the main topic of the article?**
> 這類題目就是詢問文章主旨，掌握文章大意，就可以選出答案。

What is the report mainly about?

(A) Customer satisfaction
(B) Sales results
(C) Product specifications
(D) Market trends

······ 完整題目請見 P. 025

解題技巧

- 文章主旨多半在開頭句或第一段就能略知一二。
- 這類題目還會以另一種形式出題：For whom are the instructions probably intended? 詢問「目標讀者」是誰，抓出文章主旨通常就能解題。

3. 文章目的題

What is the purpose of...?
這類題目就是詢問文章目的。

What is the purpose of the e-mail?

(A) To provide information about a foreign culture

(B) To encourage attendance for an instructive talk

(C) To remind about an overseas travel policy

(D) To report on a workshop that was conducted

完整題目請見 P. 029

解題技巧

- 文章目的通常會出現在開頭句或是結尾句。
- 另一種解題技巧，則是尋找有「為了…」含意的句子。看到如 This letter is to...（這封信是為了…）這種接在「不定詞 to V」之後的句子，通常就是答案。

4. 選項對照題

What is indicated/mentioned about...?
這類題目就是選項對照題。

What is mentioned in the e-mail?

(A) Two of the four monitors turn off almost every hour.

(B) Mike Lacey used the Ovex 42-X in his former job.

(C) Some monitors were installed in the parking lot in October.

(D) Mandy Verucci needs new monitors by the end of tomorrow.

完整題目請見 P. 037

解題技巧

- 找出選項關鍵字（如人名、地名、時間）——比對文章內容，找出一致選項。
- 若在文章中找不到該選項敘述，就是錯誤選項。
- 這類題目是基本題，雖然花時間，只要沉著對照題目與選項，就能拿分。

5. NOT 題

What is NOT mentioned about...?
這類題目就是 NOT 題。

What are visitors NOT able to do at the château?

(A) Walk in the gardens

(B) Visit all of its rooms

(C) See Louis Gerard's sculptures

(D) Enter on Thursdays

·· 完整題目請見 P. 017

解題技巧

- 這種題型跟上一類相反，選出與文章內容不一致的選項就對了。

6. 推論題

What can be inferred…?
看到有 infer、suggest 等字的題目就是推論題。

What can be inferred about the château?

(A) It is not usually open to the public.

(B) The government now owns the building.

(C) Louis Gerard did not build it.

(D) Several paintings of Louis Gerard are on display there.

·· 完整題目請見 P. 017

解題技巧

- 除了要先從文中找出相關資訊，還要能進一步推論，是比較進階的題目。

7. 同義字題

詢問文中某個單字的定義，選出語意最為接近的選項。

The word "tips" in paragraph 1, line 10, is closest in meaning to

(A) tops

(B) presents

(C) suggestions

(D) advantages

··· 完整題目請見 P. 029

解題技巧

- 選項可能是該單字的可能意思之一，請選擇「符合上下文」的選項。本題 tip 有「頂端」或「訣竅」之意，若不看上下文，就容易在選項 (A) 或 (C) 猶豫。

8. 理解意圖題

為新增題型，改制之後 Part 7 新增兩篇「文字簡訊」文章，並新增此題型，每回測驗出現 2 題，問文中某句話背後意涵。

At 11:04 A.M., what does Ms. Lewis most likely mean when she writes, "I get it"?

(A) She is in charge of picking up some items.

(B) She understands that games are useful.

(C) She knows how to use some equipment.

(D) She has figured out the meaning of a joke.

··· 完整題目請見 P. 169

解題技巧

- 需理解說話者的真正意圖，不可只看題目關鍵句就作答。本題關鍵句「I get it.」有多種解釋，光看句子本身無法作答。
- 檢視文中關鍵句的前後句，選出「符合上下文」的選項。
- 關鍵句所使用的代名詞常是解題線索，務必從上下文找出代名詞所指為何。

9. 插入句題 NEW

這類詢問某一句子該安插在文章何處的題目，為插入句題，也是新增題型，每回測驗出現 2 題。

In which of the positions marked [1], [2], [3], and [4] does the following sentence best belong? "Therefore, we have decided to update the content."

(A) [1]

(B) [2]

(C) [3]

(D) [4]

.... 完整題目請見 P. 153

解題技巧

1. 先檢視插入句。根據所提到的關鍵訊息，往回找文中重複提及的地方。
2. 插入句的代名詞或連接詞如 therefore，常是解題線索。
3. 將插入句套入文中空格，閱讀該空格的前後一句，如果語意合理有邏輯，就是答案。

10. 整合資訊題 NEW

出現在雙篇閱讀或三篇閱讀題組。多益改制後，新增「三篇閱讀」，每回測驗出 5 題 ×3 組，共 15 題，需要在不同文章中找出相關資訊並整合。

Which ticketing option listed on the Web page did Mr. Thornton use before February 1?

(A) Option 1

(B) Option 2

(C) Option 3

(D) Option 4

.... 完整題目請見 P. 211

解題技巧

1. 先找出每篇文章主旨（先看開頭一兩句），掌握文與文之間的關聯性。
2. 再看題目，推敲題目相關訊息可能會落在哪些文章裡。
3. 仔細閱讀相關段落，找出相關資訊並整合。

NOTE

職場上，講求的就是閱讀力！

— TEX 加藤

所謂英文的四大能力，就是聽、說、讀、寫。在這之中，我認為在實際職場上，最講求的就是閱讀力。

在投身多益教學之前，我曾經是商品企劃的上班族，平時需要看網路新聞，掌握國外趨勢以及國外廠商的最新動向，或是搜尋有趣商品、查看商品型錄等，否則很快就會跟不上快速的世界脈動。想在現代競爭忙碌的職場上立足，就要比競爭對手更早一步獲得最新資訊。換言之，在職場上，優異的英文閱讀力是必須的。

不僅如此，當你開始和合作對象接洽，也會碰到許多需要大量英文閱讀或是理解英文的場合。如迅速看完對方的郵件簡報並回信、查看商品功能說明書，或簽約看懂合約書等。現在網路、E-mail 與通訊軟體的普及，職場上對英文閱讀力的要求也變得越來越高。

毫無疑問，作答多益 Part 7 所需要的，就是從大量英文文章中迅速提取正確資訊的能力。多益考試這個寶庫其實彙整了許多實用的商用英文，相信各位在準備多益考試的過程中，也能大大提升自己的商務技能。

Part 1　速度訓練篇

請先達到每題 **60** 秒的速度！

CHÂTEAU BLEU OPENED FOR PUBLIC

From the beginning of June until the end of August, Château Bleu will be open to the public. This is to commemorate 200 years since the birth of important French architect and sculptor Louis Gerard, who designed and built the château as a summer residence and used it over a ten-year period toward the end of his life. Visitors will have the rare opportunity to see 17 of the 24 rooms in their original Renaissance style as well as an exhibition dedicated to his life and work. The château grounds will also be open for visitors to stroll through colorful gardens still home to some of Gerard's most notable sculptures. The château is open from 10:00 A.M. until 4:00 P.M., and the grounds are open from 10:00 A.M. until 7:00 P.M., Tuesday through Saturday. Admission is €9.00 for adults and €6.00 for students.

1. For whom is the notice most likely intended?

   (A) Sculptors

   (B) Gardeners

   (C) Curators

   (D) Tourists

2. What are visitors NOT able to do at the château?

   (A) Walk in the gardens

   (B) Visit all of its rooms

   (C) See Louis Gerard's sculptures

   (D) Enter on Thursdays

3. What can be inferred about the château?

   (A) It is not usually open to the public.

   (B) The government now owns the building.

   (C) Louis Gerard did not build it.

   (D) Several paintings of Louis Gerard are on display there.

做完之後，在下方表格填入作答時間與答對題數。

第 **1** 回 _____月_____日	第 **2** 回 _____月_____日	第 **3** 回 _____月_____日
答對題數 _____題 時間 _____分_____秒	答對題數 _____題 時間 _____分_____秒	答對題數 _____題 時間 _____分_____秒

翻譯及解析

1-3 題參考以下公告。

BLEU 城堡開放參觀

從 6 月初到 8 月底，Bleu 城堡將對外開放。這是為了紀念重要的法國建築家兼雕刻家 Louis Gerard 誕辰兩百週年。他設計並建造此城堡作為夏季居所，在他過世前的 10 年期間，都是在這裡度過。訪客可趁此難得機會，參觀 24 間當中的 17 間文藝復興時期房間，以及其生平與作品展。城堡周邊也會對外開放，訪客將能漫步在五彩繽紛的花園，這裡也放置了 Gerard 一些最著名的雕塑品。城堡開放時間為週二到週六早上 10 點到下午 4 點，周邊地區則是早上 10 點到下午 7 點。入場費成人票 9 歐元，學生票 6 歐元。

---

1. 此公告最有可能寫給誰看？

(A) 雕刻家

(B) 園丁

(C) 博物館館長

(D) 旅客

正確答案：D　　　　　　　　　　　　　　　　　　　`文章目的`

標題提到本文是 château「城堡」開放參觀的公告，換句話說，是給觀光客看的資訊，因此對象選 (D) Tourists。

①只要抓到文章目的，就能明白文章是寫給誰看。

---

2. 訪客在城堡裡不能做什麼？

(A) 在花園散步

(B) 參觀所有房間

(C) 看 Louis Gerard 的雕塑品

(D) 在週四入場

正確答案：B　　　　　　　　　　　　　　　　　　　`NOT 題`

從第 7 行 Visitors will have the rare opportunity to see 17 of the 24 rooms 可知，24 間房間只有 17 間開放參觀，並非所有房間都開放，答案為 (B)。

3. 關於城堡，從文中可推論出何事？

(A) 不常對外開放。

(B) 建築物現為政府所有。

(C) 不是由 Louis Gerard 所建造。

(D) 好幾幅 Louis Gerard 畫作在此展示。

正確答案：A　　　　　　　　　　　　　　　　　　　　　**推論題**

本題要選出符合城堡的敘述。從開頭句 From the beginning of June until the end of August, Château Bleu will be open to the public. 可知，這間城堡僅在特定期間開放參觀，故答案為 (A)。

ⓘ 這類「infer 推論題」的難度較高，要先找到相關細節再進行推論。不過這題倒是輕鬆，因為文章開頭句就和 (A) 呼應，馬上就能找出答案。第 8 行的 rare opportunity「難得的機會」也是線索。

單字

- notice *(n.)* 公告
- château *(n.)*（法文）宅邸，城堡
- be open to the public 開放大眾參觀
- commemorate *(v.)* 紀念；慶祝
  (n.) commemoration 紀念（儀式）
- architect *(n.)* 建築家
  (n.) architecture 建築
- sculptor *(n.)* 雕塑家
  (n.) sculpture 雕塑品
- be home to ～的發源地
- residence *(n.)* 住所，居住地
  (n.) resident 居民
  (v.) reside 居住

- rare *(adj.)* 稀少的
- opportunity *(n.)* 機會
- exhibition *(n.)* 展示
- be dedicated to 致力於
- stroll *(v.)* 散步
- notable *(adj.)* 知名的
- admission *(n.)* 入場費
- adult *(n.)* 成年人
- be intended for 打算，作為
- curator *(n.)*（博物館，圖書館）館長
- infer *(v.)* 推論
- on display 展示中

To: Brick First Real Estate
From: Michelle Carter
Subject: Exeter Apartment
Date: Tuesday, March 17

I took a look at a few ads on your Web site yesterday, and I'd like to inquire about apartments in the Exeter area. I'm particularly interested in the two-bedroom apartment at 32 Mellor Road. I am currently living in Sydney but will be moving to Adelaide in early May. The property in Exeter is close to the office I'll be working in, so its location would be ideal for me. I'm going to Adelaide on March 25 to meet my new employer, so I was hoping you could show me the place the next morning. If it's not available then, I'd like information on other properties in that area or in Ethelton.
Please let me know if seeing the apartment on Thursday is possible, and thank you for your time.

Michelle Carter

4. What can be inferred about Michelle Carter?

    (A) She will visit Brick First Real Estate's office in Sydney.

    (B) She is living in an apartment in Exeter.

    (C) She has found a job in Adelaide.

    (D) She does not have any interest in properties in Ethelton.

5. When does Michelle Carter wish to visit Brick First Real Estate?

    (A) March 16

    (B) March 17

    (C) March 25

    (D) March 26

6. Where did Michelle Carter find the information about the apartment?

    (A) A real estate magazine

    (B) A listing in a newspaper

    (C) An ad on the Internet

    (D) A flyer in Adelaide

做完之後，在下方表格填入作答時間與答對題數。

第 1 回 ＿＿月＿＿日	第 2 回 ＿＿月＿＿日	第 3 回 ＿＿月＿＿日
答對題數 ＿＿＿題 時間 ＿＿＿分＿＿＿秒	答對題數 ＿＿＿題 時間 ＿＿＿分＿＿＿秒	答對題數 ＿＿＿題 時間 ＿＿＿分＿＿＿秒

翻譯及解析

> 收件人：Brick 第一不動產
> 寄件人：Michelle Carter
> 主旨：伊克斯特公寓
> 日期：3 月 17 日星期二
>
> 我昨天在貴網站看到幾則廣告，想約看幾間伊克斯特區的公寓。我最有興趣的是位於梅勒路 32 號的兩房公寓。我現在住在雪梨，即將在 5 月初搬到阿德雷德區。伊克斯特區的物件距離我即將工作的地方很近，所以位置對我來說很理想。我會在 3 月 25 日去阿德雷德區跟我的新員工碰面，希望隔天上午能參觀這一區。如果這個物件已售出，請提供該區其他物件資訊給我，埃塞爾頓區的物件也可。請回覆我本週四是否方便看房，感謝您撥空閱讀此信。

4. 關於 Michelle Carter，文中可推測出什麼事情？

(A) 她將拜訪位於雪梨的 Brick 第一不動產。

(B) 她現在住在伊克斯特區的公寓。

(C) 她已經在阿德雷德找到工作。

(D) 她對埃塞爾頓區的物件沒興趣。

正確答案：C　　　　　　　　　　　　　　　　詢問細節＋推論題

需找出與本文相符的選項。從第 5 行 I... will be moving to Adelaide in early May. The property in Exeter is close to the office I'll be working in 可知，寄信人 5 月搬到了 Adelaide，開始在那裡工作。另外，從第 9 行的 I'm going to Adelaide on March 25 to meet my new employer 可知這是一份新工作，答案是 (C)。

ⓘ 本題要先逐一對照選項與內文，比較耗時，需沉著答題，接著透過隱晦的線索推測答案，是要特別小心的題型。這題就要從「搬到 Adelaide」、「該物件距離我即將工作的地方很近」，到「在 Adelaide 跟我的新員工碰面」3 項資訊推論答案。

5. Michelle Carter 希望何時拜訪 Brick 第一不動產？

(A) 3 月 16 日   (B) 3 月 17 日

(C) 3 月 25 日   (D) 3 月 26 日

正確答案：D   `詢問細節`

第 9 行提到 I'm going to Adelaide on March 25 to meet my new employer, so I was hoping you could show me the place the next morning. ，可看出寄信人想在 3 月 25 日的隔天早上參觀房子，答案是 (D)。

6. Michelle Carter 是在哪裡找到公寓資訊的？

(A) 不動產雜誌   (B) 報紙廣告

(C) 網路廣告   (D) 阿德雷德區的傳單

正確答案：C   `詢問細節`

這類寫信給對方「詢問資訊」的內容，在開頭就會闡明是從「何處」獲得資訊，這封電子郵件也不例外。開頭句 I took a look at a few ads on your Web site yesterday, and I'd like to inquire about apartments in the Exeter area. 說明寄信人是在 Web site「網站」看到廣告。答案是換句話說的 (C) An ad on the Internet。

ⓘ 這類在選項將內文改寫的「換句話說」題，是多益 Part 7 常見考法。

單字

- real estate 不動產
- subject *(n.)* 主旨
- ad *(n.)* 廣告，advertisement 的縮寫
- inquire *(v.)* 詢問
  (n.) inquiry 詢問
- apartment *(n.)* 公寓
- particularly *(adv.)* 尤其，特別
- be interested in 對～有興趣
- currently *(adv.)* 目前

- property *(n.)* 房產，物件
- location *(n.)* 地點
- ideal *(adj.)* 理想的
- employer *(n.)* 雇主
  (n.) employee 員工
  (n.) employment 雇用
  (v.) employ 雇用
- available *(adj.)*（房子）空出來的
- flyer *(n.)* 傳單

Results from our customer satisfaction survey conducted at retail stores selling our 6DX Digi-Pact show an overall high level of satisfaction with this product. The survey was done over a six-month period beginning in April this year, four months after the camera's release. Nearly 90% of those surveyed said they were satisfied with its price, usability, and appearance, and more than 60% noted that the camera's autofocus function was its top feature. Picture quality also scored high on the survey, as did its performance for taking high-quality photographs in both bright and dim lighting. Only battery life received an average rating on the survey. From these results, and considering satisfaction leads to recommendation, we can expect to sell more of this product in its first year on the market than the number of 5DX model units sold since its release two years ago.

7. What is the report mainly about?

(A) Customer satisfaction

(B) Sales results

(C) Product specifications

(D) Market trends

8. What is NOT mentioned as an attractive feature of the camera?

(A) Design

(B) Focusing function

(C) Durability

(D) Photo quality

9. For how long was the survey conducted?

(A) Three months

(B) Four months

(C) Five months

(D) Six months

做完之後，在下方表格填入作答時間與答對題數。

第 1 回 ＿＿月＿＿日	第 2 回 ＿＿月＿＿日	第 3 回 ＿＿月＿＿日
答對題數 ＿＿題 時間 ＿＿分＿＿秒	答對題數 ＿＿題 時間 ＿＿分＿＿秒	答對題數 ＿＿題 時間 ＿＿分＿＿秒

翻譯及解析

> 我們在販售 6DX Digi-Pact 的零售店做了顧客滿意調查，結果顯示，顧客對這項產品的整體滿意度是高的。這項調查是在今年 4 月初，也就是相機上市後 4 個月開始進行，長達半年期間。近九成受訪者表示，他們對售價、操作便利度以及外觀很滿意，超過六成的人認為自動對焦是最大特色。這台相機的成像品質，以及在高低光源都能拍到高品質相片也獲得高分。只有電池壽命獲得一般評價。根據以上數據，並且考量滿意度已達到推薦，我們可以預期，這項產品在市場第 1 年的銷售，將會高於 5DX 在兩年前上市至今的銷售。

7. 本報告主要是關於什麼？

(A) 客戶滿意度 　　　　　　　(B) 銷售結果
(C) 產品規格 　　　　　　　　(D) 市場趨勢

正確答案：A　　　　　　　　　　　　　　　　　　　**文章主旨**

本文是顧客滿意度調查的結果，因此此答案是 (A) Customer satisfaction。其他選項也出現在文中，但仔細閱讀就會發現與文意不合，是 Part 7 常見陷阱。結尾雖然提及預期銷售，但並不等於 Sales results「銷售結果」。雖然文章有關於 product 的敘述，但並非說明 Product specifications「產品規格」。最後出現 market 一詞，但並不是指 Market trends「市場趨勢」。

8. 以下何者並非該相機的吸睛特點？

(A) 設計 　　　　　　　　　　(B) 對焦功能
(C) 待機時間 　　　　　　　　(D) 成像品質

正確答案：C　　　　　　　　　　　　　　　　　　　**NOT 題**

選出文中未提及的吸睛特點。(A) Design，(B) Focusing function 與 (D) Photo quality 分別呼應第 9 行的 appearance「外觀」，第 10 行的 autofocus function「自動對焦」以及第 11 行的 picture quality「成像品質」，且第 7 行敘述消費者對上述各項功能是滿意的。(C) Durability 雖然有呼應第 14 行的 battery life「電池壽命」，但消費者的反應僅止於 average rating「一般評價」，所以不算是 attractive feature。

9. 這項調查為期多久？

(A) 三個月

(B) 四個月

(C) 五個月

(D) 六個月

正確答案：D

詢問細節

題目問 how long，所以要找與「期間」相關的資訊。從第 4 行的 The survey was done over a six-month period，period 為「期間」之意，答案是 (D)。

單字

- customer satisfaction 顧客滿意度
- survey *(n.)/(v.)* 調查
- conduct *(v.)* 執行
- retail store 零售店
- overall *(adj.)* 整體的
  (adv.) overall 整體上
- release *(n.)* 上市，推出
  (v.) release 發售
- nearly *(adv.)* 幾乎
- be satisfied with 對～感到滿意
- usability *(n.)* 好用，操作順手
- appearance *(n.)* 外表
- feature *(n.)* 特色
- quality *(n.)* 品質
- score high 獲得高分
- performance *(n.)* 性能；表演
- dim *(adj.)* 暗的
- battery life 電池壽命
- average *(adj.)* 平均的
- consider *(v.)* 考慮
- lead to 導致，促成
- recommendation *(n.)* 推薦
  (v.) recommend 推薦
- expect *(v.)* 期待，預期
- mainly *(adv.)* 主要
- product specifications 產品規格
- market trend 市場趨勢
- mention *(v.)* 提及
- durability *(n.)* 耐用度
  (adj.) durable 耐用的

Dear Mr. Bradford:

We will be giving a workshop for those who will be posted in Brazil for the first time. Living in a foreign country can be quite challenging so having a well of information to draw from is important for your success and comfort overseas. We would like you to join the workshop, which will be rich with valuable information and held on January 31 from 13:00 to 17:00 in the meeting room on the second floor. During the workshop, many topics will be covered such as tips for learning Portuguese, information on Brazilian culture and etiquette, schooling for children, and strategies for making your life easier while you are away from home. Spouses are also welcome and encouraged to attend the workshop. If you are unable to attend, please contact Mr. Hudson in personnel so he can arrange an individual session.

Allyson Burwell

10. What is the purpose of the e-mail?

    (A) To provide information about a foreign culture

    (B) To encourage attendance for an instructive talk

    (C) To remind about an overseas travel policy

    (D) To report on a workshop that was conducted

11. The word "tips" in paragraph 1, line 10, is closest in meaning to

    (A) tops

    (B) presents

    (C) suggestions

    (D) advantages

12. What can be inferred about Mr. Bradford?

    (A) He has been responsible for a seminar.

    (B) He has been promoted recently.

    (C) He has attended a workshop with his wife.

    (D) He has never worked in Brazil before.

做完之後，在下方表格填入作答時間與答對題數。

第1回 ＿＿月＿＿日	第2回 ＿＿月＿＿日	第3回 ＿＿月＿＿日
答對題數 ＿＿題 時間 ＿＿分＿＿秒	答對題數 ＿＿題 時間 ＿＿分＿＿秒	答對題數 ＿＿題 時間 ＿＿分＿＿秒

翻譯及解析

親愛的 Bradford 先生：

我們將會替首次被派遣去巴西的人舉行研習會。旅居國外是相當具挑戰性的事情，若有豐富資訊能參考，對於海外成功與居住舒適是至關重要。我們想邀請您參加此研習會，會中將提供許多寶貴資訊，於 1 月 31 日下午 1 點到 5 點在二樓會議廳舉行。會中將討論許多主題，包含學葡萄牙文的訣竅、巴西文化與禮儀資訊、當地幼兒教育，以及讓國外生活更加容易的方法。我們也很歡迎並鼓勵攜伴參加。如果您無法參加，請聯繫人事的 Hudson 先生，他會替您安排個別講習。

Allyson Burwell

10. 此電子郵件的目的為何？

(A) 提供外國文化資訊　　　　　(B) 鼓勵參加教育座談
(C) 提醒一項海外出差政策　　　(D) 回報舉辦過的研習會

正確答案：B　　　　　　　　　　　　　　　　　　　　**文章目的**

開頭句 We will be giving a workshop 點出要舉辦研習會一事，並且說明研習內容，因此電子郵件目的是 (B)。

11. 第一段第 10 行的 tip 一字，意思最接近

(A) tops「頂端」　　　　　　　(B) presents「禮物」
(C) suggestions「建議」　　　　(D) advantages「優點」

正確答案：C　　　　　　　　　　　　　　　　　　　　**同義字題**

第一段第 10 行的 tips 出現在 many topics will be covered such as tips for learning Portuguese... 一句，意為「有幫助的建議」，因此與 (C) suggestions 最接近。tip 除了有「訣竅，建議」之意，也有「小費」，「尖端」等意思。常見的片語 the tip of the iceberg 指的就是「冰山一角」。

ⓘ 同義字題經常使用該字的其他定義作為陷阱選項，需根據前後文語意來作答。

12. 關於 Bradford 先生，從文中可以推論出什麼？

(A) 他負責一場研習會。

(B) 他最近升官。

(C) 他跟他老婆參加了一場研習會。

(D) 他從沒去過巴西。

正確答案：D　　　　　　　　　　　　　　　　　　　**推論題**

Mr. Bradford 是這封電子郵件的收件者。從開頭句 We will be giving a workshop for those who will be posted in Brazil for the first time. 可知，收到這封研習會簡介的 Mr. Bradford 也是第一次派駐巴西，答案是 (D)。

ⓘpost 在這裡當動詞，指「委派」。

單字

- post (v.) 委派，派駐
- challenging (adj.) 有挑戰性的
- well of information 大量資訊
- draw (v.) 獲取
- comfort (n.) 舒適
  (adj.) comfortable 舒服的
- overseas (adv.) 在海外
  (adj.) overseas 海外的
- be rich with 富含～
- valuable (adj.) 有價值的
- cover (v.) 涵蓋，包括
- etiquette (n.) 禮儀
- strategy (n.) 策略
- spouse (n.) 配偶
- encourage (v.) 鼓勵

- attend (v.) 參加，出席
  (n.) attendance 出席
- contact (v.) 聯絡
- personnel (n.) 人事
- individual (adj.) 個別的，個人的
  (n.) individual 個人
- purpose (n.) 目的
- instructive (adj.) 具教育意義的，具啟發性的
- remind (v.) 提醒
- travel (v.)/(n.) 出差；旅遊
- policy (n.) 政策
- advantage (n.) 優點
- responsible (adj.) 有責任的，負責～的
- promote (v.) 晉升
- recently (adv.) 最近

Sales Manager Position at TekSelect

TekSelect Manufacturing, a Canadian-based company, is seeking a sales manager to join its dynamic team. The manager will be responsible for the Asia-Pacific region. This is a permanent position. Requirements include exceptional presentation skills, 3-plus years previous management experience, proficiency in communication and writing, experience in the corporate environment as well as attention to detail and pride in one's work. The successful candidate will work at our Vancouver headquarters but must be willing to travel and relocate to one of our branch offices in Hong Kong, South Korea, Singapore, or Thailand. Candidates must speak at least one Asian language, and experience in sales is preferred. Send your résumé to hiring@tekselect.com with one reference pertinent to management engagement.

13. What is stated as a requirement of the job being advertised?

    (A) Familiarity with applications
    (B) Willingness to travel
    (C) Ability to speak three languages
    (D) Prior job experience in sales

14. What is the applicant required to submit?

    (A) A presentation
    (B) An e-mail address
    (C) A reference
    (D) A language certificate

15. In which country is the headquarters of TekSelect Manufacturing located?

    (A) Canada
    (B) South Korea
    (C) Singapore
    (D) Thailand

做完之後，在下方表格填入作答時間與答對題數。

第 1 回 ＿＿＿月＿＿＿日	第 2 回 ＿＿＿月＿＿＿日	第 3 回 ＿＿＿月＿＿＿日
答對題數 ＿＿＿題 時間 ＿＿＿分＿＿＿秒	答對題數 ＿＿＿題 時間 ＿＿＿分＿＿＿秒	答對題數 ＿＿＿題 時間 ＿＿＿分＿＿＿秒

翻譯及解析

13-15 題請參考以下廣告。

> ## TekSelect 徵銷售經理
>
> Tekselect 製造公司是總部位於加拿大的公司，現正尋找一名銷售經理加入他們充滿活力的團隊。此經理將負責亞太地區，為正式職缺。職缺條件為出色的簡報技巧，3 年以上管理經驗，精通溝通與寫作，有在企業環境工作的經驗，對工作細心且有榮譽感。錄取者將在溫哥華總部工作，要有出差意願且願意轉調至香港、南韓、新加坡或泰國分公司。應徵者須至少會一門亞洲語言，有銷售經驗更好。請將履歷連同一封有管理經驗人士的推薦信寄到 hiring@tekselect.com。

13. 以下何者為本職缺的必備條件？

(A) 熟悉軟體　　　　　　　　　(B) 願意出差

(C) 能説 3 門語言　　　　　　　(D) 先前有銷售經驗

正確答案：B　　　　　　　　　　　　　選項對照

這份工作的 requirement「必備條件」就羅列在第 5 行的 Requirements include 之後，第 12 行的 must be willing to travel 則呼應選項 (B)。

ⓘ 文中雖提及 experience in sales，但此條件僅是 preferred「有的話更好」，並非必要，所以 (D) 不符。

14. 申請者必須提交什麼？

(A) 一份簡報　　　　　　　　　(B) 電子郵件地址

(C) 一封推薦信　　　　　　　　(D) 一門語言證照

正確答案：C　　　　　　　　　　　　　選項對照

應徵者被要求寄送的東西出現在信件最後一句：Send your résumé to hiring@tekselect. com with one reference pertinent to management engagement. 其中的 reference「推薦信」剛好呼應選項 (C)。

ⓘ「推薦函」除了說 reference 外，還可以說 letter of reference，reference letter，recommendation 以及 letter of recommendation。

15. TekSelect 製造公司的總部位於哪個國家？

(A) 加拿大

(B) 南韓

(C) 新加坡

(D) 泰國

正確答案：A 詢問細節

這題詢問的是 headquarters「公司總部」所在地。從開頭句 TekSelect Manufacturing, a Canadian-based company 可知，公司總部設在加拿大，答案為 (A)。

ⓘ 只要知道 Canadian-based 也指「總部設在加拿大」，就不難解題。

單字

- advertisement *(n.)* 廣告
  (v.) advertise 打廣告
- position *(n.)* 職位
- dynamic *(adj.)* 充滿活力的
- region *(n.)* 區域
  Asia-Pacific region 亞太區域
- permanent position 正式職缺
- requirement *(n.)* 必備條件
- exceptional *(adj.)* 出色的，優異的
- previous *(adj.)* 先前的
- management experience 管理經驗
- proficiency *(n.)* 精通
- corporate *(adj.)* 公司企業的
- environment *(n.)* 環境
- successful candidate 錄取者
- headquarters *(n.)* 總部
  （恆加 s，單複數同型）

- relocate *(v.)* 搬遷，搬家
- preferred *(adj.)* 更好的，更合意的
- résumé *(n.)* 履歷
- reference *(n.)* 推薦信
- be pertinent to 關於～
- engagement *(n.)* 從事
- state *(v.)* 陳述
- requirement *(n.)* 必備條件
  (v.) require 要求，規定
- application *(n.)* 應用程式
- prior *(adj.)* 先前的
- applicant *(n.)* 申請者
- submit *(v.)* 提交，繳交
- certificate *(n.)* 證書，證照
- located *(adj.)* 位於～的

To: Jake Durham
From: Mandy Verucci
Subject: New Monitors
Date: November 5

Dear Mr. Durham:

We need eight new monitors for the security room. Ted Jones from security told me that two of the four we are currently using have been malfunctioning over the last two weeks, and one of them switches off every hour or so. The other two still work but are old and will likely have their own problems before long. Also, considering last month's installment of extra security cameras in the parking lot and inventory room, we need additional monitors to better cover the scope of our surveillance. Mike Lacey suggested we go with Ovex monitors. According to him, they are handier than the type we use now and come with a number of functions designed specifically for security purposes. He used the Ovex 42-X monitor in a previous job and thinks it is the ideal model for us. They cost $620 apiece, so I need your signature on the purchase request form I faxed to you earlier this week. I would appreciate your signing it before noon tomorrow, as I need to place the order as soon as possible.

Best Regards,
Mandy Verucci

16. What is the purpose of the e-mail?

(A) To promote a product

(B) To warn security

(C) To request approval

(D) To complain about facilities

17. Who will order the Ovex 42-X monitors?

(A) Jake Durham

(B) Mandy Verucci

(C) Mike Lacey

(D) Ted Jones

18. What is mentioned in the e-mail?

(A) Two of the four monitors turn off almost every hour.

(B) Mike Lacey used the Ovex 42-X in his former job.

(C) Some monitors were installed in the parking lot in October.

(D) Mandy Verucci needs new monitors by the end of tomorrow.

做完之後，在下方表格填入作答時間與答對題數。

第 1 回 _____月_____日	第 2 回 _____月_____日	第 3 回 _____月_____日
答對題數 _____題 時間 _____分_____秒	答對題數 _____題 時間 _____分_____秒	答對題數 _____題 時間 _____分_____秒

翻譯及解析

16-18 題參考以下電子郵件。

收件人：Jake Durham

寄件人：Mandy Verucci

日期：11 月 5 日

親愛的 Durham 先生：

警衛室需要 8 台新螢幕。保全人員 Ted Jones 告訴我，目前 4 台螢幕有 2 台在兩週前故障，其中 1 台每幾個小時就自行關機。剩下 2 台雖然正常運作，但已經老舊，不久可能會出現問題。此外，考量上個月才在停車場與倉庫架設新攝影機，我們需要更多螢幕才能涵蓋更多監視範圍。Mike Lacey 建議我們使用 Ovex 螢幕。他說 Ovex 螢幕比我們目前所使用的型號更方便操作，安全用途的功能也更多。他在前一份工作用過 Ovex 42-X 的螢幕，覺得這個型號很適合我們。這款監視器一台要價 620 元，我在本週已傳真請款單過去，你需要在上面簽名，因為我得儘快下單採購，如果你能在明天中午前簽好，我會非常感激。

Mandy Verucci

---

16. 此電子郵件的目的為何？

(A) 促銷產品

(B) 提出安全警告

(C) 請求批准

(D) 抱怨設施

正確答案：C　　　　　　　　　　　　　　　　　　　　　　　文章目的

開頭句 We need eight new monitors for the security room. 表明需要購買新螢幕一事，接著說明目的與預計購買的機種，再提出 I need your signature on the purchase request form，要求簽名允許採購。因此文章目的是 (C)。

ⓘ這題比較困難，因為目的放在本文最後，需看完整篇文章才會知道。

17. 誰會訂購 Ovex 42-X 螢幕？

(A) Jake Durham

(B) Mandy Verucci

(C) Mike Lacey

(D) Ted Jones

正確答案：**B**

詢問細節

題目的 order 是解題關鍵字，從最後一句 I need to place the order as soon as possible 可知，寄件者 Mandy Verucci 會負責訂購螢幕，答案是 (B)。

ⓘ 作答時需知道題目的 order the Ovex 42-X monitors，就是文中 place the order 的換句話說。

18. 電子郵件中提到了什麼？

(A) 4 台螢幕中有 2 台幾乎每小時就關機。

(B) Mike Lacey 在前一份工作用過 Ovex 42-X。

(C) 10 月才在停車場安裝螢幕。

(D) Mandy Verucci 在明天前要拿到新螢幕。

正確答案：**B**

選項對照

選出與本文內容一致的選項。第 11 行提到 Mike Lacey suggested we go with Ovex monitors... He used the Ovex 42-X monitor in a previous job，答案是 (B)。

單字

- security (n.) 保全人員
- currently (adv.) 目前
- malfunction (v.)/(n.) 故障
- switch off 關閉電源 = turn off
- before long 不久之後
- installment (n.) 安裝
  (v.) install 安裝
- extra (adj.) 額外的
- security camera 監視攝影機
- inventory (n.) 倉庫
- additional (adj.) 額外的
- cover (v.) 涵蓋
- surveillance (n.) 監視
- go with 選擇，搭配
- according to 根據
- handy (adj.) 方便的
- specifically (adv.) 特地，專門地

- apiece (adv.) 每個
- signature (n.) 簽名
  (v.) sign 簽名
- purchase request form 採購單
- appreciate (v.) 感激
- place an order 下訂單，購買
- as soon as possible 越快越好
- promote (v.) 宣傳，促銷
- warn (v.) 警告
- request (v.) 請求
- approval (n.) 核可，通過
  (v.) approve 核准
- complain (v.) 抱怨
  (n.) complaint 抱怨
- facility (n.) 設施
- turn off 關閉電源
- former (adj.) 先前的

NOTE

To all employees:

_____

As was announced in November, our pay period will change from this month. Until the end of last year, payday was the last Friday of the month. From this month, you will be paid on the second and fourth Fridays of the month. Because of this change, the amount per paycheck will be less, but your monthly and yearly income will not be affected. Payslips will be available each payday and can be picked up as usual from the payroll department. Remember to make sure your work schedule is filled in on a weekly basis and includes any overtime hours or absence from work. In case of absence, work schedules can be filled in and submitted online in the same way as before. If you have any questions regarding these changes, please speak with Mr. Orson in payroll.

19. For whom is the notice most likely intended?

    (A) Company employees

    (B) Professional accountants

    (C) Mr. Orson

    (D) Business clients

20. What is the purpose of the notice?

    (A) To notify about changes in the payroll system

    (B) To publicize new services for clients

    (C) To explain the up-to-date accounting system

    (D) To encourage attendance at upcoming workshops

21. What is indicated in the notice?

    (A) Payslips will only be available at the end of the month.

    (B) An announcement was already made in December.

    (C) Work schedules are no longer available online.

    (D) Employees will receive less money per paycheck.

做完之後，在下方表格填入作答時間與答對題數。

第 1 回 ＿＿＿月＿＿＿日	第 2 回 ＿＿＿月＿＿＿日	第 3 回 ＿＿＿月＿＿＿日
答對題數 ＿＿＿題 時間 ＿＿＿分＿＿＿秒	答對題數 ＿＿＿題 時間 ＿＿＿分＿＿＿秒	答對題數 ＿＿＿題 時間 ＿＿＿分＿＿＿秒

翻譯及解析

19-21 題參考以下公告。

致全體員工：

如同先前在 11 月公布的，公司發薪週期將從本月起更改。直到去年年底，薪資發放日一直是每個月最後一個星期五。從本月開始，各位將會在每月第 2 與第 4 個週五收到薪資。由於這項改變，各位每次收到的薪資會減少，但月薪及年度總薪資將不會受到影響。如同以往，薪資明細可在發薪日當天於薪資部門取得。記得每週務必填寫工作日誌、加班與缺勤時數。若有缺勤狀況，工作日誌可於線上填寫並提交。關於以上變更，若有任何問題，請聯絡薪資部門的 Orson 先生。

19. 此公告最有可能寫給誰看？

(A) 公司員工
(B) 專業會計師
(C) Orson 先生
(D) 公司客戶

正確答案：A　　　　　　　　　　　　　　文章主旨

先掌握文章大意，才能推敲出文章是寫給誰看。這篇是發薪日異動的公告，由此可知公告對象是員工，答案是 (A)。

ⓘ文章主旨題是基本題，較為簡單，請務必拿分。

20. 此公告的目的為何？

(A) 通知薪資給付方式的變更
(B) 向客戶宣傳新服務
(C) 說明最新會計系統
(D) 鼓勵出席研討會

正確答案：A　　　　　　　　　　　　　　文章目的

本文主旨是發薪日異動，因此撰寫目的是為了通知員工，答案是 (A)。

21. 此公告提及什麼？

(A) 只有在月底才能取得薪資明細。

(B) 12 月已經發過公告。

(C) 再也無法在線上取得工作日誌。

(D) 員工每次領到的薪水會減少。

正確答案：D	選項對照

選出與內文一致的選項。從第 6 行的 the amount per paycheck will be less 可知，每次領取的薪水會減少，也就是 (D)。

ⓘ 這類題目需一一對照選項與文章內容，需細心作答。

單字

- announce *(v.)* 宣布

  (n.) announcement 通知，公告
- pay period 發薪週期
- payday *(n.)* 發薪日
- amount *(n.)* 金額
- paycheck *(n.)* 薪水
- income *(n.)* 收入
- affect *(v.)* 影響
- payslip *(n.)* 薪資條，薪資明細
- as usual 照常
- payroll department 薪資部門
- make sure 確保
- fill in 填寫
- on a weekly basis 每週

- overtime *(n.)* 加班
- absence *(n.)* 缺勤

  (adj.) absent 缺席的
- in case of 在～狀況下
- regarding *(prep.)* 關於
- accountant *(n.)* 會計人員
- client *(n.)* 顧客
- notify *(v.)* 告知
- publicize *(v.)* 公布；宣傳
- explain *(v.)* 解釋
- up-to-date *(adj.)* 最新的
- accounting system 記帳系統
- upcoming *(adj.)* 即將舉行的
- indicate *(v.)* 指出

∾ GREEN LEAF ∾
AGRICULTURAL SUPPLIES

April 25

Ms. Eva Leone
2275 Jackson Drive
Philadelphia, PA 19122

Dear Ms. Leone:

We are very sorry about the delay in delivering your Green Leaf equipment, especially because you paid the extra $35 express delivery fee on top of the normal shipping charge of $15. After receiving your letter, I called the delivery company and asked that they look into the matter. I learned that several packages were held up en route through Chicago Westport Airport. Apparently, the container in which your package was being delivered contained other parcels that were carrying contraband. The entire container was held up at customs for a week of thorough inspection. We would like to guarantee that this never happens again, though such matters, as you can imagine, are out of our hands. Nevertheless, you should have been notified immediately about the delay, and for that reason we will refund the extra fee in full. As a token of our good faith, we would like to offer you a $50 discount voucher you can use on a future purchase. Thank you for your continued patronage.

Brandon Hoff

Brandon Hoff
Green Leaf Agricultural Supplies

22. What did Brandon Hoff do after Eva Leone contacted him?

(A) Sent her a new package

(B) Called the airport in Chicago

(C) Requested a product number

(D) Contacted a delivery company

23. How much of a discount will Eva Leone get on her next purchase?

(A) $15

(B) $35

(C) $50

(D) $85

24. What caused the delay?

(A) Severe weather in Chicago

(B) Incorrect information on the invoice

(C) An unexpected inspection at customs

(D) A careless oversight by the supplier

做完之後，在下方表格填入作答時間與答對題數。

第 **1** 回 ＿＿月＿＿日	第 **2** 回 ＿＿月＿＿日	第 **3** 回 ＿＿月＿＿日
答對題數 ＿＿題 時間 ＿＿分＿＿秒	答對題數 ＿＿題 時間 ＿＿分＿＿秒	答對題數 ＿＿題 時間 ＿＿分＿＿秒

翻譯及解析

22-24 題參考以下信件。

~綠葉~
農產設備

4 月 25 日
Eva Leone 小姐
19122 賓州費城傑克森大道 2275 號

親愛的 Leone 小姐：

延誤寄送您所訂購的綠葉裝備，我們感到十分抱歉，尤其您還支付比一般運費 15 元多 35 元的快遞費用。收到您的來信後，我致電給貨運公司，請他們調查此事，得知運送途中有幾件包裹被扣留在芝加哥西港機場。載有您包裹的貨櫃似乎含有違禁品。整個貨櫃被扣留在海關一週，正在進行詳細檢查。我們很想向您保證這件事不會再發生，但如您所知，這種事情實在非我們能控制。然而，您早該收到我們的延遲通知，為此，我們會全額退還您多支付的運費。為了表示誠意，在此提供 50 元折價券，供您在下次購物使用。謝謝您持續惠顧。

Brandon Hoff
綠葉農產設備

22. Eva Leone 聯繫 Brandon Hoff 之後，他做了什麼？

(A) 寄給她新包裹
(B) 打電話到芝加哥的機場
(C) 要求產品編號
(D) 聯繫貨運公司

正確答案：D

詢問細節

Brandon Hoff 是這封信的寄件人，Eva Leone 是收信人，這點可從題目 after Eva Leone contacted him 這個關鍵句確認。接著在第 4 行 After receiving your letter, I called the delivery company and asked that they look into the matter. 可知，答案是 (D) Contacted a delivery company。

① 一看到文章是信件，就要先確認寄件人與收信人姓名，這是基本功。

23. Eva Leone 下次購物可享有多少折扣？

(A) 15 元

(B) 35 元

(C) 50 元

(D) 85 元

正確答案：C 詢問細節

題目的 discount 是關鍵字。倒數兩行提到 we would like to offer you a $50 discount voucher you can use on a future purchase. 答案是 (C)。

ⓘ 用 discount 這個線索來搜尋整篇文章，就能找出答案。

- -

24. 是什麼原因導致延誤？

(A) 芝加哥天候惡劣

(B) 發票資訊錯誤

(C) 海關意外檢查

(D) 供應商疏忽漏寄

正確答案：C 詢問細節

題目關鍵字為 caused，詢問寄件延遲的原因。第 8 行的 Apparently, the container in which your package was being delivered contained other parcels that were carrying contraband. The entire container was held up at customs for a week of thorough inspection. 就有說明，可推斷答案是 (C)。

ⓘ contraband 一字，字首 contra- 是 against「反對」的意思，字尾 -band 則有 ban「禁令」之意，合起來就是「違反禁令」，即「違禁品」。

單字

- agricultural *(adj.)* 農業的
  (n.) agriculture 農業
- supplies *(n.)* 供給品（常用複數）
  (n.) supplier 供應商
- delay *(n.)* 延誤
- deliver *(v.)* 遞送
  (n.) delivery 遞送
- equipment *(n.)* 設備
- express delivery 快遞
- on top of 除了～之外，還有
- normal *(adj.)* 一般的
- shipping charge 運費
- look into 調查
- hold up 耽擱，延誤
- en route / enroute *(adv.)* 途中
- apparently *(adv.)* 似乎，看來
- container *(n.)* 貨櫃
- parcel *(n.)* 包裹
- contraband *(n.)* 違禁品，走私品

- customs *(n.)* 海關（恆用複數）
- thorough *(adj.)* 仔細徹底的
- inspection *(n.)* 檢查
  (v.) inspect 檢查
- guarantee *(v.)* 保證
- out of one's hands 不受控制的
- immediately *(adv.)* 立刻
- refund *(v.)/(n.)* 退款
- as a token of 作為～的表示
- good faith 誠意
- discount voucher 折價券
- purchase *(n.)/(v.)* 購買（物）；購買
- patronage *(n.)* 光顧
- severe weather 惡劣天候
- incorrect *(adj.)* 錯誤的
- invoice *(n.)* 發票
- unexpected *(adj.)* 出乎意料的
- oversight *(n.)* 失察，疏忽

NOTE

INTERACTIONS: A MARV GABLE MASTERPIECE

What can I say about Marv Gable's new book *Interactions*? In short, buy it! Merely borrowing it or browsing through it is not enough, as you will want to read it more than once.

* * *

Gable's newest release is a compelling and reader-friendly surprise that draws energy to the recently dull and colorless self-help genre. Aiming to reach a wider range of readers, the author examines relationships inside and outside the office in his new book. With an insight and sense of humor that are highly profound, Gable succeeds in identifying commonalities among relationships between family members and friends as well as superiors and subordinates. What makes some relationships succeed and others fail? Gable again endeavors to answer this question as he did in *The Individual's Tribe*. And pursuing answers to this question, he believes, is something that all people should do to strengthen relationships from personal to professional.

* * *

If you are in any sort of relationship, have had one, or plan on having one, then *Interactions* is a must-read.

25. How does the reviewer describe the book *Interactions*?

    (A) It is popular.
    (B) It is professional.
    (C) It is short.
    (D) It is funny.

26. The word "dull" in paragraph 2, line 2, is closest in meaning to

    (A) blunt
    (B) overcast
    (C) meticulous
    (D) uninteresting

27. What is indicated about Marv Gable?

    (A) He works in a large office.
    (B) He is an award-winning author.
    (C) He is a well-known fiction writer.
    (D) He has written about relationships before.

做完之後，在下方表格填入作答時間與答對題數。

第 **1** 回 ＿＿＿月＿＿＿日	第 **2** 回 ＿＿＿月＿＿＿日	第 **3** 回 ＿＿＿月＿＿＿日
答對題數 ＿＿＿題 時間 ＿＿＿分＿＿＿秒	答對題數 ＿＿＿題 時間 ＿＿＿分＿＿＿秒	答對題數 ＿＿＿題 時間 ＿＿＿分＿＿＿秒

翻譯及解析

《互動》：MARV GABLE 又一傑作

對於 Marv Gable 的新書《互動》，我還能說什麼呢？總之，買就對了！光是隨意翻閱，或瀏覽一次根本不夠，因為你將會一看再看！

* * *

Gable 的新作既扣人心弦，也是相當易讀的驚喜之作，替近來無趣且黯淡無光的自我成長類型書注入活力。為了引起更廣大讀者的共鳴，作者在新書中檢視辦公室由內而外的人際關係。Gable 透過深刻的洞察力與幽默感，成功定義了家人朋友與上司下屬兩者間的共同點。是什麼決定一段關係的成敗？Gable 再次致力於回答這個問題，如同他先前在《個體部落》一書所做的。他深信，為了強化個人與職場關係，人人都應該找出這個問題的答案。

* * *

不管你正在一段關係當中，曾經有過一段關係，或是即將進入一段關係，這本《互動》是你必讀之作。

---

25. 評論者如何敘述《互動》一書？

(A) 大受歡迎。

(B) 專業。

(C) 簡短。

(D) 有趣。

正確答案：D　　　　　　　　　　　詢問細節

題目的關鍵字是 how，要找出這篇書評是如何形容本書。第二段第 5 行 With an insight and sense of humor that are highly profound 可知，這是有趣的書，答案是 (D) It is funny.

ⓘ 文中的 sense of humor that is highly profound「具強烈的幽默感」，在選項中換句話說，改用 funny 表達。

26. 第二段第 2 行 dull 一字，意思最接近

(A) blunt「鈍的」

(B) overcast「多雲陰暗的」

(C) meticulous「嚴謹的」

(D) uninteresting「無趣的」

正確答案：D　　　　　　　　　　　　　　　同義字題

dull 出現在 energy to the recently dull and colorless self-help genre 一句中，表示「無聊的，無趣的」，跟 (D) uninteresting 同義。

ⓘ dull 可當「（刀子）鈍的，不鋒利的」，意思等同 (A) blunt。也有「（天氣）陰暗的」之意，意同 (B) overcast。此外也有「反應遲鈍的」，「（顏色）暗淡的」的意思。

....

27. 關於 Marv Gable，本文提到什麼？

(A) 他在大公司上班。

(B) 他是得獎作家。

(C) 他是知名小說作家。

(D) 他寫過人際關係相關書籍。

正確答案：D　　　　　　　　　　　　　　　選項對照

從第二段第 9 行的 What makes some relationships succeed and others fail? Gable again endeavors to answer this question as he did in *The Individual's Tribe*. 可知，他已經出版過有關人際關係的書，答案是 (D)。

ⓘ 從本文的 as he did in *The Individual's Tribe*，可推斷他在其他著作也做一樣的事。也就是說，他已經試圖回答過問題，而那個問題就是文章第 13 行的 What makes some relationships succeed and others fail?

單字

- review (n.) 評論
  (v.) review 評論
  (n.) reviewer 評論者
- interaction (n.) 互動
- masterpiece (n.) 傑作
- browse (v.) 瀏覽
- compelling (adj.) 引人注意的
- reader-friendly (adj.) 易讀的
- draw energy 注入活力
- recently (adv.) 最近
- dull (adj.) 無聊的
- self-help (adj.) 自我提升的
- genre (n.) 類型，體裁
- aim to 以～為目標
- reach (v.) 到達
- author (n.) 作者
- examine (v.) 分析
- relationship (n.)（人際）關係
- insight (n.) 洞察力
- a sense of humor 幽默感
- profound (adj.) 強烈的；深刻的

- identify (v.) 定義；確認
- commonality (n.) 共通性
- superior (n.) 上司
  (adj.) superior 優於的
- subordinate (n.) 下屬
- fail (v.) 失敗
- endeavor (v.) 竭盡全力
- tribe (n.) 部落
- pursue (v.) 追求
- strengthen (v.) 加強
- personal (adj.) 個人的
- professional (adj.) 職業的；專業的
- must-read (n.) 必讀作品
- blunt (adj.)（刀子）鈍的
- overcast (adj.)（天候）多雲陰暗的
- meticulous (adj.) 嚴謹的
- uninteresting (adj.) 無趣的
- award-winning (adj.) 得獎的
- well-known (adj.) 有名的
- fiction (n.) 小説

NOTE

To: Staff
From: Doug Sinclair
Subject: Project Reports
Date: August 16

This message is sent to those who have yet to submit their project reports. The deadline is today; however, at the very latest they should be sent to me by e-mail or put on my desk before noon tomorrow. Keep in mind that your report does not have to be very detailed; a brief summary describing your project and project goals will suffice. You should also indicate how far you have come in your project and fill out the proposed schedule section of the template, which is attached to this e-mail and available as hardcopy from your supervisors. All projects should be wrapped up before the end of the fiscal year; though, in some cases extensions can be given. If you need an extension, come by my office so we can figure something out. Regardless, I'll be going over all of your reports this week, so get them to me soon.

Regards,

Doug Sinclair

28. What is the purpose of the memo?

    (A) To remind recipients about a deadline

    (B) To report on the progress of a project

    (C) To notify about completion of a project

    (D) To request the extension of a deadline

29. What are the recipients asked to do?

    (A) Inform about the status of their current project

    (B) Write a detailed description of their work

    (C) Come in early the following morning

    (D) Submit a proposal for a presentation

30. What can be inferred from the memo?

    (A) The memo was sent to all employees.

    (B) The deadline for the report has already passed.

    (C) The report must be submitted by e-mail.

    (D) There is a fixed template for the report.

做完之後，在下方表格填入作答時間與答對題數。

第 1 回 ＿＿＿月＿＿＿日	第 2 回 ＿＿＿月＿＿＿日	第 3 回 ＿＿＿月＿＿＿日
答對題數 ＿＿＿題 時間 ＿＿＿分＿＿＿秒	答對題數 ＿＿＿題 時間 ＿＿＿分＿＿＿秒	答對題數 ＿＿＿題 時間 ＿＿＿分＿＿＿秒

翻譯及解析

28-30 題參考以下備忘錄。

收件人：全體員工
寄件人：Doug Sinclair
主旨：提案報告
日期：8 月 16 日

這則訊息是給尚未繳交提案的人。期限是今天，不過最晚在明天中午前給我，用電子郵件寄送或放我桌上皆可。請記住，報告不用交代太多細節，只需簡要敘述報告與報告目標即可。各位也需指出報告執行進度，並填寫報告格式上的預計進度表，報告格式隨附在此郵件中，也可以向主管索取紙本。

所有提案應在本會計年度前總結，若有特例可以延長。需要延期的人，來辦公室找我，我們一起想辦法。儘管如此，我打算在這週看完所有報告，所以儘早給我。

Doug Sinclair

28. 本備忘錄的目的為何？

(A) 提醒收件人截止期限　　(B) 報告提案進度
(C) 通知提案完成　　(D) 請求延長期限

正確答案：A　　`文章目的`

文章開頭提到 This message is sent to those who have yet to submit their project reports. The deadline is today，因此這封信的目的是 (A) To remind recipients about a deadline。

ⓘ memo 翻成「備忘錄」，是公司用來內部聯繫用的「內部通知信」。

29. 收件人被要求要做什麼？

(A) 告知目前提案狀況　　(B) 撰寫詳細工作內容
(C) 隔天提早到公司　　(D) 繳交簡報提案

正確答案：A　　`選項對照`

題目關鍵字為 recipient「收件人」與 asked「被要求」，第 7 行的 You should also indicate how far you have come in your project 用了 should 一字，表示這是公司對員工的請求，答案為 (A)。

30. 從備忘錄中可以推論出什麼？

(A) 備忘錄是寄給全體員工。

(B) 報告截止日已經過了。

(C) 報告須透過電子郵件繳交。

(D) 報告有固定格式。

正確答案：D　　　　　　　　　　　　　　　　　　**推論題**

從第 9 行的 and fill out the proposed schedule section of the template 的 template 「範本」可知，報告有固定格式，答案是 (D)。開頭句 This message is sent to those who have yet to submit their project reports 可知，這封內部通知只寄給還沒交報告的人，所以選項 (A) 錯誤。

單字

- memo *(n.)* 公司內部通知，備忘錄
- staff *(n.)* 全體員工
  （集合名詞，需與複數動詞連用）
- project *(n.)* 提案，專案
- deadline *(n.)* 截止期限
- at the (very) least 至少
- however *(adv.)* 然而
- keep in mind that 記住～
- detailed *(adj.)* 詳細的
  (n.) detail 詳細
- brief *(adj.)* 簡要的
- summary *(n.)* 概要，大綱
- suffice *(v.)* 足夠
- fill out/in 填寫
- propose *(v.)* 提出
  (n.) proposal 提案
- template *(n.)* 範本

- attach *(v.)* 附加
- hardcopy *(n.)* 紙本
- wrap up 完成，總結
- fiscal year 會計年度 = financial year
- extension *(n.)* 延長
  (v.) extend 延長
- come by 順道拜訪
- figure out 想出（辦法）
- regardless *(adv.)* 儘管如此
- go over 仔細查看
- remind *(v.)* 提醒
- recipient *(n.)* 收件者
- progress *(n.)* 進度，進展
- completion *(n.)* 完成
- inform *(v.)* 通知
- status *(n.)* 狀況

To: Claire Smith
From: Lucas Mendel
Subject: 420-GC Packaging
Date: March 25

Sales figures for our new coffee maker have continued to be disappointing. After going over issues that came up in a customer survey, we have found that the main problem lies not with the product but with its packaging. Although the new package is lighter, both customers and retailers are dissatisfied with its design. First, it is difficult to carry because most of the coffee maker's weight inside the package favors one side. This likely explains why so many of the products are being dropped at stores. Second, the color of the package is not good. Because it is white, it easily gets dirty and can look stained by the time it reaches store shelves. Third, storing the product is difficult because of the curved back of the package and its sloped top. The rectangular shape we discussed last year is better.

We need to change the package design before the next round of coffee makers is manufactured in April. The pictures on the front of the package are good, so let's keep them, but the ones on the side are too small. I expect the marketing division to send me some fresh design ideas by the end of this week so that we can get started.

Best regards,

Lucas Mendel

31. What is the e-mail mainly about?

    (A) A defective product

    (B) A sales forecast

    (C) An instruction booklet

    (D) A package design

32. The word "issues" in paragraph 1, line 3, is closest in meaning to

    (A) positions

    (B) problems

    (C) choices

    (D) versions

33. What can be inferred about the coffee maker?

    (A) It is currently very popular among customers.

    (B) There was a discussion about the packaging last year.

    (C) There have been some customer complaints about its quality.

    (D) It will not be produced until the beginning of May.

做完之後，在下方表格填入作答時間與答對題數。

第 1 回 ＿＿＿月＿＿＿日	第 2 回 ＿＿＿月＿＿＿日	第 3 回 ＿＿＿月＿＿＿日
答對題數 ＿＿＿＿題 時間 ＿＿＿分＿＿＿秒	答對題數 ＿＿＿＿題 時間 ＿＿＿分＿＿＿秒	答對題數 ＿＿＿＿題 時間 ＿＿＿分＿＿＿秒

翻譯及解析

31-33 題參考以下電子郵件。

收件人：Claire Smith
寄件人：Lucas Mendel
主旨：420-GC 的包裝
日期：3 月 25 日

我們新推出的咖啡機銷售數字持續令人失望。查看完顧客調查提到的問題之後，發現最大問題是在包裝上，而非產品本身。雖然新的包裝較輕，然而消費者與零售商對設計並不滿意。首先，這個設計難以搬運，因為此包裝造成咖啡機大部分重量偏向一邊。這可能也說明為何多數店內陳設商品常掉下來。第二，包裝顏色不好。因為是白色包裝，很容易弄髒，放在架上銷售之前就有髒污。第三，存放商品不易，因為包裝的背後是曲線，頂部是斜的。去年我們討論的長方形包裝比較好。

我們要在 4 月製造下一批咖啡機之前更換包裝。包裝正面圖片很棒，可以保留。不過側面圖片太小張。我希望市場部門在本週五之前，寄給我一些新穎的設計點子，我們才能開始進行。

---

31. 此電子郵件主要是關於什麼？

(A) 瑕疵商品
(B) 銷售預估
(C) 使用手冊
(D) 包裝設計

正確答案：D　　　　　　　　　　　　　　　　　　　　　　　文章主旨

第一段第 4 行提到 the main problem lies not with the product but with its packaging. Although the new package is lighter, both customers and retailers are dissatisfied with its design. 表示包裝設計有問題，並指出具體的問題點。因此這封郵件與 (D) 有關。

① 遇到文章主旨題，也不要忽略信件主旨欄（Subject:）。本文主旨欄寫著「Subject: 420-GC Packaging」，光看標題也能推測答案。

32. 第一段第 3 行的 issue 一字，意思最接近

(A) positions「位置」　　　　(B) problems「問題」
(C) choices「選擇」　　　　　(D) versions「版本」

正確答案：B　　　　　　　　　　　　　　　　**同義字**

第一段第 3 行的 issues 出現在 After going over issues that came up in a customer survey」一句中，因此意思與 (B) problems「問題」較接近。

ⓘ issue 除了當「問題」之外，也有「（雜誌）期號」、「議題」、「發行物」等意思。
另外也可以當動詞，有「發布，發行」等意思。

33. 關於咖啡機，從文中可以推論出什麼？

(A) 目前相當受到消費者歡迎。　　(B) 去年曾討論過包裝一事。
(C) 有些客訴抱怨品質不好。　　　(D) 到 5 月初才會再生產。

正確答案：B　　　　　　　　　　　　　　　　**推論題**

從第一段最後的 The rectangular shape we discussed last year is better. 可知，去年有討論過包裝設計，答案是 (B)。

單字

- packaging (n.) 包裝方式
  (n.) package 包裝
- sales figure 銷售數字
- disappointing (adj.) 令人失望的
- issue (n.) 問題
- lie (v.) （問題或責任）在於
- customer (n.) 消費者
- retailer (n.) 零售商
- be dissatisfied with 對～不滿
- weight (n.) 重量
- favor (v.) 偏好
- stained (adj.) 弄髒的
- by the time 在～時間之前

- store (v.) 儲存
- curved (adj.) 曲線的
- sloped (adj.) 斜的
- rectangular (adj.) 長方形的
- discuss (v.) 討論
- manufacture (v.) 大量製造
- division (n.) 部門
- defective (adj.) 有瑕疵的
- forecast (n.)/(v.) 預測，當動詞時三態同型
- instruction booklet 說明小冊子
- version (n.) 版本
- among (prep.) 在～之間（用於三者以上）
- not A until B 直到 B 才 A

Halifax Recycle, the only cell phone and computer recycling shop in Halifax, has served the community for 20 years. We take any computer, monitor, printer, fax machine, or cell phone you bring to our door, and at no charge.* We even offer FREE pick-up for large quantities. Because your electronics contain hazardous materials, let our experts, who care about the Earth, dispose of or recycle them. If you would like us to make a pick-up or have any questions, do not hesitate to contact us. We are located between the Alston Factory Outlet Mall and Leo's Upholstery on Laurier Avenue.

FOR A MAP WITH OUR LOCATION, VISIT:
www.halifaxyclemap.com
E-MAIL: info@halifaxycle.ca
PHONE: 1-555-773-1258

*Due to new regulations for disposal of copper and aluminum material parts, we will be charging a fee for disposal of all CRT monitors beginning on May 1

34. According to the advertisement, what can be found on the company's Web site?

(A) A price list
(B) A safety regulation
(C) A disposal request form
(D) A store location

35. What item will require fees for disposal after May 1?

(A) Computer hardware
(B) Cell phones
(C) Fax machines
(D) CRT monitors

36. What is NOT indicated about Halifax Recycle?

(A) It has been in business for 20 years.
(B) It has specialists who handle dangerous disposal.
(C) It has a promotion running until the end of April.
(D) It has no competitors in Halifax.

做完之後，在下方表格填入作答時間與答對題數。

第 1 回 _____月_____日	第 2 回 _____月_____日	第 3 回 _____月_____日
答對題數 _____題 時間 _____分_____秒	答對題數 _____題 時間 _____分_____秒	答對題數 _____題 時間 _____分_____秒

翻譯及解析

Halifax 回收是 Halifax 區唯一收手機與電腦的回收店,在這個社區已經服務 20 個年頭。我們回收你帶來的所有電腦、螢幕、印表機、傳真機以及手機,而且不收取任何費用。* 我們甚至提供大型器具免費到府收取服務。您的電器產品可能含有危險物質,因此,就讓本店關心地球的專業人員來執行丟棄或回收事宜。如需我們上府收件,或有其他問題,請聯繫我們。本店位於勞瑞爾大道上,Alston 工廠暢貨中心與 Leo 家飾用品店中間。

> **本店地圖請見網站:**
> www.halifaxyclemap.com
> E-MAIL: info@halifaxycle.ca
> **電話:** 1-555-773-1258

* 丟棄銅鋁製品相關法規已更新,5 月 1 日起,我們將對所有映像管螢幕酌收處理費用。

---

34. 根據廣告,官網上可以找到什麼?

(A) 價目表   (B) 安全法規
(C) 廢棄物清理表格   (D) 店面位置

正確答案:D   選項對照

題目的 the company's Web site「官網」是解題關鍵字。從灰底的 FOR A MAP WITH OUR LOCATION, VISIT: www.halifaxyclemap.com 可知,網站上有店面地圖,答案是 (D)。

---

35. 哪項商品從 5 月 1 日開始要收費?

(A) 電腦硬體   (B) 手機
(C) 傳真機   (D) 映像管螢幕

正確答案:D   詢問細節

題目的 fees「費用」是解題關鍵字,正好呼應廣告下方所備註的 we will be charging a fee for disposal of all CRT monitors beginning on May 1.,答案是 (D)。

ⓘ這種打星號的備註資訊常是出題所在,文章若有出現備註,請務必看完。

36. 關於 Halifax 回收，以下何者沒有提及？

(A) 已經經營 20 年。　　　　　　　(B) 有專門人士處理危險廢棄物。

(C) 4 月底前有促銷方案。　　　　　(D) 在 Halifax 沒有競爭同業。

正確答案：C　　　　　　　　　　　　　　　　　　**NOT 題**

選出與內容不符的選項。(A) It has been in business for 20 years. 呼應第一段第 1 行的 Halifax Recycle... has served the community for 20 years.。(B) It has specialists who handle dangerous disposal. 呼應第一段第 6 行的 Because your electronics contain hazardous materials, let our experts, who care about the Earth, dispose of or recycle them.。(D) It has no competitors in Halifax. 則是呼應第一段第 1 行的 Halifax Recycle, the only cell phone and computer recycling shop in Halifax。只有 (C) It has a promotion running until the end of April. 未呼應文中任何敘述，(C) 是答案。

ⓘhazardous 與 dangerous 都是「危險的」的意思。

單字

- recycle *(v.)* 回收利用
- serve *(v.)* 提供服務
- community *(n.)* 社區
- at no charge 免費
- pick-up *(n.)* 領取（某物）；接送（某人）
- quantity *(n.)* 數量
- electronics *(n.)* 電器
- contain *(v.)* 包含
- hazardous *(adj.)* 危險的
- material *(n.)* 材料
- expert *(n.)* 專家
- dispose *(v.)* 清除，丟棄（+ of）
  (n.) disposal of ～的丟棄物
- hesitate *(v.)* 猶豫
- upholstery *(n.)* 家飾品
- avenue *(n.)* 大道

- due to 由於
- regulation *(n.)* 規定
- copper *(n.)* 銅
- aluminum *(n.)* 鋁
- fee *(n.)* 費用
- according to 根據
- location *(n.)* 地點
- item *(n.)* 品項
- require *(v.)* 需要
- hardware *(n.)* 硬體
- in business 營業中的
- specialist *(n.)* 專家
- handle *(v.)* 處理
- promotion *(n.)* 促銷
- run *(v.)* 營運；運轉；進行
- competitor *(n.)* 競爭者

To: All Staff
From: Sarah Lawrence
Subject: Company Banquet
Date: November 10

The annual company banquet will be held on Saturday, December 12. Family members, including children, are welcome to come along, and tickets can be purchased from Shane Lee in personnel. The ticket price is $75; children 12 and under do not need a ticket. Our usual venue at the Barnes Hotel is undergoing renovations this year, so the banquet will be at the Marlton Hotel on Finch Drive. Ted Fellows and Lisa Wakowski have already started planning for the occasion and would like anyone interested in volunteering to get a hold of them. Several people are needed to fill posts on December 12, such as ticket collectors and coat check staff as well as people to decorate the hall. Please contact Ted or Lisa as soon as possible if you are interested in helping out before the banquet. The hotel's expert chefs will be preparing a lot of great food, so make sure to come with an appetite!

Sarah Lawrence
Vice President

37. What is the purpose of the memo?

    (A) To encourage employees to buy movie tickets
    (B) To announce a new company policy
    (C) To advertise new services at a hotel
    (D) To notify employees about an upcoming event

38. Who should employees contact about paying for tickets?

    (A) Sarah Lawrence
    (B) Lisa Wakowski
    (C) Shane Lee
    (D) Ted Fellows

39. What is NOT true about the banquet?

    (A) The company is soliciting volunteers for the preparations.
    (B) It will be held at the same hotel as the previous year.
    (C) The company will hire outside help for the food.
    (D) It does not require any admission for children under twelve.

做完之後，在下方表格填入作答時間與答對題數。

第 1 回 ＿＿月＿＿日	第 2 回 ＿＿月＿＿日	第 3 回 ＿＿月＿＿日
答對題數 ＿＿＿題 時間 ＿＿＿分＿＿＿秒	答對題數 ＿＿＿題 時間 ＿＿＿分＿＿＿秒	答對題數 ＿＿＿題 時間 ＿＿＿分＿＿＿秒

翻譯及解析

37-39 題參考以下備忘錄。

收件人：全體員工
寄件人：Sarah Lawrence
主旨：公司聚餐
日期：11 月 10 日

年度員工聚餐將在 12 月 12 日星期六舉辦。歡迎攜家帶眷，餐券可以找人事部門的 Shane Lee 購買。入場票一張 75 元，12 歲以下孩童不需購買。我們往年去的場地 Barnes 飯店今年整修，所以改在芬奇大道上的 Marlton 飯店舉行。Ted Fellows 與 Lisa Wakowski 已經著手準備這場盛事，想徵求有興趣的同仁義務幫忙。目前還需要幾名人手協助 12 月 12 日當天事宜，如收取餐券，協助衣物寄放以及會場布置。有意願在聚餐前幫忙的同仁，請儘快聯繫 Ted 或 Lisa。飯店專業主廚將會準備豐盛美味餐點，務必攜帶良好食慾前來！

Sarah Lawrence
副總

37. 此備忘錄目的為何？

(A) 鼓勵員工購買電影票
(B) 宣布公司新政策
(C) 宣傳飯店新服務
(D) 通知員工即將舉行的活動

正確答案：D　　　　　　　　　　　　　　文章目的

文章開頭就提到 The annual company banquet will be held on Saturday, December 12. ，接著說明詳情，目的是 (D)。

38. 員工該找誰買票？

(A) Sarah Lawrence
(B) Lisa Wakowski
(C) Shane Lee
(D) Ted Fellows

正確答案：C　　　　　　　　　　　　　　詢問細節

題目 paying for tickets 是解題關鍵字。從第 3 行的 and tickets can be purchased from Shane Lee in personnel. 可知 Shane Lee 負責販售票券，答案是 (C)。

ⓘ 選項 (C) 以外的人名雖然也出現在文中，但都不是負責販售票券的人。只要冷靜作答就不會掉入陷阱。

39. 關於聚會，以下何者為非？

(A) 公司正在徵求自願幫忙準備的人。

(B) 在去年同一場地舉行。

(C) 公司將會請其他業者準備餐點。

(D) 12 歲以下孩童不需入場費。

正確答案：**B**　　　　　　　　　　　　　　　NOT 題

選出與內容不一致的選項。(A) The company is soliciting volunteers for the preparations. 呼應第 8 行的 Ted Fellows and Lisa Wakowski have... to decorate the hall.。(C) The company will hire outside help for the food. 呼應最後兩行的 The hotel's expert chefs will be preparing a lot of great food, so make sure to come with an appetite!。(D) It does not require any admission for children under twelve. 則呼應第 5 行的 children 12 and under do not need a ticket.。唯獨 (B) It will be held at the same hotel as the previous year. 與第 5 行的 Our usual venue at the Barnes Hotel is undergoing renovations this year, so the banquet will be at the Marlton Hotel on Finch Drive. 文意不符，因此是答案。

ⓘsolicit 其實就是 ask for「請求」的意思，是多益常考單字。

單字

- banquet *(n.)* 宴會
- annual *(adj.)* 每年的
  (adv.) annually 每年
- venue *(n.)* 會場
- undergo *(v.)* 歷經
- renovation *(n.)* 改裝，翻修
  (v.) renovate 翻修
- occasion *(n.)* 特殊場合或事宜

- volunteer *(v.)/(n.)* 自願服務；志願者
- get a hold of 聯絡
- several *(adj.)* 數個的
- post *(n.)* 職缺
- ticket collector 收票員
- decorate *(v.)* 裝飾
- appetite *(n.)* 食慾
- solicit *(v.)* 請求

BOSTON PHOTO
Your studio for the journey of your life

BOSTON PHOTO is excited to announce it will be reopening its doors on June 19. The studio, one of the longest-running businesses in the city and the oldest photography store in Massachusetts, was closed last year after a fire on the second floor of the building. Boston Photo's owner, Mallory Reese, whose great-grandfather, Samuel Albert, first opened the shop, will continue to run the business. Known for its high-quality portraits and portfolio that includes several Boston mayors and other high-profile Bostonians, as well as its reputation for always offering exceptional rates, the shop is eagerly anticipating the return of its customers. After the fire, the studio was closed for nearly a year. But Ms. Reese continued to employ all five of her staff and work with clients outside the shop. Boston Photo will be at the same spot it has been for nearly a century, at 24 Rutherford Street on the first floor of the Rideau Building.

Visit its Web site at **www.bostonphoto.click.com** to see the store's comprehensive portfolio and unbeatable rates.

40. What does this announcement publicize?

(A) An established business

(B) A newly opened store

(C) A location change

(D) A Web site renewal

41. What is indicated about Boston Photo?

(A) It is the oldest company in Massachusetts.

(B) It has a dozen skilled staff.

(C) It accepts online reservations.

(D) It offers services at reasonable prices.

42. What is NOT mentioned in the announcement?

(A) Samuel Albert is related to Mallory Reese.

(B) Boston Photo has been open for nearly one hundred years.

(C) The fire started in the photo studio last year.

(D) Services outside the studio were never interrupted.

做完之後，在下方表格填入作答時間與答對題數。

第 1 回 _____月_____日	第 2 回 _____月_____日	第 3 回 _____月_____日
答對題數 _____題 時間 _____分_____秒	答對題數 _____題 時間 _____分_____秒	答對題數 _____題 時間 _____分_____秒

翻譯及解析

40-42 題參考以下公告。

波士頓照相館
為您記錄生活軌跡的攝影室

我們很開心宣布，波士頓照相館即將在 6 月 19 日重新開幕。這家相館是全市最老字號的店家之一，也是全麻州最古老的相館。去年因為大樓二樓大火，停業一年。本館將由店主 Mallory Reese 繼續經營。她的曾祖父 Samuel Albert 是這家相館的創始者。這家相館以好幾任波士頓市長以及當地士紳的高品質肖像及攝影集聞名，同時價格也是出了名的實惠，因此相當期待顧客再次光臨。大火之後，此相館休息將近一年時間，不過，Reese 小姐與全部 5 名員工仍持續在外服務客戶。波士頓相館將會在經營已近一世紀的原址繼續營業，店址是羅瑟福街 24 號 Rideau 大樓一樓。

請上網站 www.bostonphoto.click.com 查看本館各類攝影作品，以及無人能及的實惠價格。

40. 此公告在宣傳什麼？

(A) 知名店家　　　　　　　　(B) 新開店家
(C) 位址變更　　　　　　　　(D) 網站更新

正確答案：A　　　　　　　　　　　　　　　　　　　**文章主旨**

這篇文章旨在傳達相館重新開幕的資訊，並且說明店家特色。因此，宣傳的是 (A)。publicize 是「宣傳」的意思，與 advertise 同義。established 原意是「已經建立的」，在此延伸有「知名的」的意思。

41. 關於波士頓相館，文中指出什麼？

(A) 是麻州最老的公司。　　　　(B) 擁有 12 名熟練員工。
(C) 接受線上預約。　　　　　　(D) 以合理價格提供服務。

正確答案：D　　　　　　　　　　　　　　　　　　　**選項對照**

從第 11 行的 offering exceptional rates 和最後一行的 unbeatable rates 可知，相館收費相當便宜，與選項 (D) 對應。rate 在多益中常作為「價格」之意。

ⓘ 此外，文中第 2 行 one of the longest-running businesses，是指歷史最悠久的公司「之一」，而非「最」悠久的，因此選項 (A) 錯誤。

42. 此公告沒有提到什麼？

(A) Samuel Albert 跟 Mallory Reese 有血緣關係。

(B) 波士頓相館已經營業近一百年。

(C) 去年該相館發生火災。

(D) 相館外出服務從沒中斷過。

正確答案：C　　　　　　　　　　　　**NOT ＋ 推論題**

選出與本文內容不符的選項。從第 4 行的 last year after a fire on the second floor of the building. 可知去年大樓二樓曾發生火警。此外，從第一段最後 1 行的 Boston Photo will be at the same spot it has been for nearly a century, at 24 Rutherford Street on the first floor of the Rideau Building. 可知相館開在大樓 1 樓。綜合上述，可推斷火災發生地點並非相館，選項 (C) 不符。

ⓘ 本題難度較高，需利用已知資訊做進一步推論。

單字

- studio *(n.)*（攝影室或錄音室等）工作室
- longest-running business 老字號店家
- portrait *(n.)* 肖像
- portfolio *(n.)* 攝影集；作品集
- mayor *(n.)* 市長
- high-profile *(adj.)* 知名的
- reputation *(n.)* 名譽
- rate *(n.)* 價格
- eagerly *(adv.)* 熱切地
- anticipate *(v.)* 期待
- comprehensive *(adj.)* 全面的
- unbeatable *(adj.)* 無法超越的

- publicize *(v.)* 宣傳
- established *(adj.)* 已確立的；知名的
- newly opened 新開幕的
- renewal *(n.)* 更新，翻新
- accept *(v.)* 接受
- dozen *(n.)* 12 個，一打
- reservation *(n.)* 預約
  (v.) reserve 預約
- reasonable price 合理價格
- be related to 與～有血緣關係
- interrupt *(v.)* 中斷；打擾
  (n.) interruption 中斷；打擾

To: Andy Sulong
From: Elias Jayasuriya
Subject: Training
Date: Wednesday, May 6

Dear Andy:

I'm writing to make a couple of additional requests for next week's training program in Kuala Lumpur. But first I want you to know how pleased we are to have a team of sales representatives based in Malaysia joining our team this year. We intend to help you make the program a success in any way we can, as the trainees will soon be on the frontline of communications with our customers there.

I believe you have already started preparing for the program by arranging for a venue, renting equipment, and selecting training materials. Regarding equipment, could you make sure that I will be able to connect my laptop to the projector? During the morning session, I will need to show two promotional videos.

Also, if it is not too late, I would like several pages included in the training manual. If you have already bound the materials, I can print the additional pages here in Bangkok and bring them with me. However, I'd rather not have to take them on the flight. Ideally, a staff member on your end can prepare them and have them bound with the rest of the manual. Please let me know if this is possible. That is all for now. I look forward to seeing you in Kuala Lumpur.

Best regards,

Elias Jayasuriya
Department Chief
Human Resources

43. Who is the training for?

    (A) Computer technicians

    (B) Newly hired staff

    (C) Sales executives

    (D) Human resources personnel

44. What does Elias Jayasuriya ask Andy Sulong to do?

    (A) Pick him up at the airport

    (B) Lend him a laptop computer

    (C) Show videos to the trainees

    (D) Add extra pages to a manual

45. What is indicated about the program?

    (A) The trainees will handle customers in Thailand.

    (B) The preparations are already in progress.

    (C) Promotional videos will be shown in the afternoon.

    (D) It will take place at the end of May in Malaysia.

做完之後，在下方表格填入作答時間與答對題數。

第 1 回 ＿＿＿月＿＿＿日	第 2 回 ＿＿＿月＿＿＿日	第 3 回 ＿＿＿月＿＿＿日
答對題數 ＿＿＿題 時間 ＿＿＿分＿＿＿秒	答對題數 ＿＿＿題 時間 ＿＿＿分＿＿＿秒	答對題數 ＿＿＿題 時間 ＿＿＿分＿＿＿秒

翻譯及解析

43-45 題參考以下電子郵件。

收件人：Andy Sulong
寄件人：Elias Jayasuriya
主旨：訓練
日期：5 月 6 日星期三

親愛的 Andy：

寫信給你是有關下週吉隆坡的訓練課程，想向你提出兩三點額外請求。但首先，我想讓你知道，馬來西亞總部的銷售團隊能在今年加入我們公司，我們感到相當開心。因為受訓者馬上就要成為和客戶面對面的一線人員，因此，我們會盡一切努力，協助你成功進行這場課程。

我想你已經著手準備安排場地、租借器材，以及挑選教材等事。關於器材一事，你可以確認筆電是否有辦法連接投影機嗎？因為我在上午課程會播放兩部宣傳影片。

此外，如果來得及的話，我想新增教材頁面。如果你已經裝訂好，我可以先在曼谷印出新增頁面，直接帶過去。不過可以的話，我是希望不要帶這些資料搭飛機。理想的作法是，你那裡的工作人員幫我準備好新增頁面，並跟原本的教材裝訂在一起。請讓我知道這樣是否可行。目前就先這樣，期待在吉隆坡見到你。

Elias Jayasuriya
人力資源部主任

43. 訓練對象是誰？

(A) 電腦工程師
(B) 新進員工
(C) 銷售經理
(D) 人力資源部員工

正確答案：B

詢問細節

從第一段第 3 行的 a team of sales representatives based in Malaysia joining our team this year. 可知，即將有新銷售團隊加入公司，而透過第一段的內容可推論，這場研習是為了他們而舉辦，答案是 (B)。

44. Elias Jayasuriya 要求 Andy Sulong 做什麼？

(A) 去機場接他

(B) 借他一台筆電

(C) 給受訓者看影片

(D) 增加使用手冊頁數

正確答案：D　　　　　　　　　　　　　　選項對照

Elias Jayasuriya 是這封信的寄件人，Andy Sulong 則是收件者。Elias 在第三段第 1 行寫到，I would like several pages included in the training manual.，向 Andy 提出想增加手冊頁數的請求，答案是 (D)。

ⓘ 題目出現 ask to do，是與「請求」相關的題目，因此文中與「請求」有關的句子就是答題線索。這類內容常出現在文章後半部，可留意最後一段的內容。

- -

45. 關於課程，本文提到什麼？

(A) 受訓者將負責泰國客戶。

(B) 已經在準備中。

(C) 宣傳影片會在下午播放。

(D) 5 月底會在馬來西亞舉行。

正確答案：B　　　　　　　　　　　　　　選項對照

第二段第 1 行提到 I believe you have already started preparing for the program by arranging for a venue, renting equipment, and selecting training materials.，因此答案是 (B)。

ⓘ 其中 you have already started preparing for the program 這句，可知課程準備已經開始，正好呼應選項的 in progress「進行中」。

單字

- a couple of 兩、三個
- additional *(adj.)* 額外的
- pleased *(adj.)* 感到喜悅的
- sales representative 銷售員
- based in 總部位於
- trainee *(n.)* 受訓者
  (n.) trainer 訓練者
- frontline *(adj.)*
  前線的;直接與客戶面對面的
- communication *(n.)* 溝通
- arrange *(v.)* 安排
- projector *(n.)* 投影機
- rent *(v.)/(n.)* 租借;租金

- equipment *(n.)* 器材,設備
- material *(n.)* 教材
- bind *(v.)* 裝訂(過去式與過去分詞:bound)
- I'd rather 我更偏好
- rest of 其餘的
- look forward to +Ving/N 期待～
- human resources 人力資源
- technician *(n.)* 技術人員
- executive *(n.)* 主管,經理
- personnel *(n.)* 員工
- in progress 進行中
- take place 舉行

NOTE

August 1

Dear David:

This letter is to let you know that I have decided to leave
Minnesota and return to London to live with my parents at the
start of next month. There I will start working at the company's
branch office under Thomas Jefferies after a one-week vacation.
I will be happy to help transfer my job responsibilities to my
successor before I leave at the end of this month.

Eleven years with the company has been an invaluable experience
for me. I deeply appreciate your trust in giving me positions with
increasing levels of responsibility over the years, even though I did
not have experience in the industry before joining the company. In
particular, the experience I have gained in my current position as
assistant branch manager will be highly useful to me in London.

David, since my first year working here, I have strived to develop
my management abilities to match yours. You are highly respected
for your treatment of both staff and clients, and you always know
the best action to take in any situation. I sincerely hope that in the
future I become as capable a manager as you are.

I am sure you can understand that leaving Minnesota has been
a very difficult decision for me to make. Your acceptance of my
transfer will be greatly appreciated.

Yours sincerely,

Abigail Branford

Abigail Branford

46. What is the purpose of Ms. Branford's letter?

    (A) To commend an employee on his achievement

    (B) To congratulate David on his promotion

    (C) To notify David of her decision

    (D) To recommend a colleague for a position

47. The word "invaluable" in paragraph 2, line 1, is closest in meaning to

    (A) useful

    (B) previous

    (C) inevitable

    (D) worthless

48. What will Ms. Branford do in September?

    (A) She will work at her parents' company.

    (B) She will transfer her current job responsibilities.

    (C) She will work under Thomas Jefferies.

    (D) She will take a management course in London.

做完之後，在下方表格填入作答時間與答對題數。

第 1 回 ＿＿月＿＿日	第 2 回 ＿＿月＿＿日	第 3 回 ＿＿月＿＿日
答對題數 ＿＿題 時間 ＿＿分＿＿秒	答對題數 ＿＿題 時間 ＿＿分＿＿秒	答對題數 ＿＿題 時間 ＿＿分＿＿秒

46-48 題參考以下信件。

8 月 1 日

親愛的 David：

這封信是要讓您知道，我決定在下個月初離開明尼蘇達，返回倫敦與雙親同住。休完一週假之後，我會到 Thomas Jefferies 所領導的分公司就任。在月底離職前，我很樂意協助交接工作職責給繼任者。

在這裡工作 11 年的日子，對我來説是相當珍貴的經驗。我深深感激您對我的信任，即使我在加入公司之前沒有任何相關經驗，您仍在這些年交付我越來越多的職責。尤其是我在分公司副經理這個職位上所獲得的經驗，對我在倫敦的工作非常有幫助。

David，從我在這裡工作的第一年起，我就一直精進自己的管理能力，期許能與您一樣。您無論在對待員工還是與客戶應對，都相當令人尊敬，無論遇到什麼狀況，您總能做出最好的判斷。我由衷希望，在未來我也能成為像您一樣有能力的經理。

相信您能明白，離開明尼蘇達對我來説是非常艱難的決定。您若願意接受我的請調，我將會深深感激。

Abigail Branford 敬上

46. Branford 小姐寫信的目的為何？

(A) 讚揚某員工成就

(B) 恭賀 David 升官

(C) 通知 David 她的決定

(D) 推薦某同事擔任某職位

正確答案：C　　　　　　　　　　　　　　　　　文章目的

開頭句 This letter is to let you know that I have decided to leave Minnesota and return to London to live with my parents at the start of next month. 就點出目的。這裡的 you 指的是收件人 David，答案是 (C)。

47. 第二段第 1 行的 invaluable 一字，意思最接近

(A) useful「有用的」

(B) previous「珍貴的」

(C) inevitable「無法避免的」

(D) worthless「毫無價值的」

同義字題

invaluable 出現在 Eleven years with the company has been an invaluable experience for me. 一句中，與 (A) useful「有用的」的意思最接近。

① 看到字首是 in- 的單字，會直覺認為是反義詞，但 invaluable 的意思等於 valuable。精確來說，invaluable 的程度更強，有 very valuable 的意思。

48. Branford 小姐 9 月將會做什麼？

(A) 去雙親公司上班。

(B) 交接職務。

(C) 在 Thomas Jefferies 底下工作。

(D) 在倫敦上管理課程。

詢問細節

關鍵字是 September，因此要注意與時間相關的線索。信件開頭寫 August 1，表示這封信是在 8 月寫的，因此文中的 next month 指的是 September。而第一段第 2 行提到 ... return to London... at the start of next month. There I will start working at the company's branch office under Thomas Jefferies... 可知，寄信者 9 月起會在 Thomas Jefferies 的底下工作，答案是 (C)。

單字

- transfer *(v.)/(n.)* 轉移；調動
- job responsibility *(n.)* 職責；工作描述
- successor *(n.)* 繼任者
- invaluable *(adj.)* 寶貴的
- experience *(n.)* 經驗
- appreciate *(v.)* 感激
- even though 即使
- increase *(v.)/(n.)* 增加
  （動詞重音在後，名詞重音在前）
- industry *(n.)* 業界
- in particular 尤其
- gain *(v.)* 獲得
- assistant branch manager 分公司副經理
- strive to 努力～
- develop *(v.)* 發展
- match *(v.)* 使相配
- respect *(v.)/(n.)* 尊敬
- treatment *(n.)* 對待，待遇
- sincerely *(adv.)* 真誠地
- capable *(adj.)* 有能力的
- acceptance *(n.)* 接受
- commend *(v.)* 讚揚
- achievement *(n.)* 功績，成就
- congratulate *(v.)* 祝賀
- recommend *(v.)* 推薦
- colleague *(n.)* 同事
- inevitable *(adj.)* 無法避免的
- worthless *(adj.)* 毫無價值的

NOTE

To: Clifford Randall
From: Marcus Barker
Subject: Apology
Date: February 18

Dear Mr. Randall:

I apologize for not contacting you sooner about the extension and understand you have been waiting to hear from us since our January meeting three weeks ago. We tried sending you an e-mail immediately after the meeting, but after getting your message yesterday, we realized you did not get it. I looked into the matter and found that when renovations were being done at our office from mid-January to early February, we had several problems with our server, and e-mails that we had thought were being sent were actually being lost. Along with the message we tried sending you was a draft of the estimate, which is attached to this message. After you go over it, please call me at 555-0942 and let me know if you find the price agreeable. And once we settle on that, I will come by your place with a copy of the contract. Again, I'm sorry for the delay, and I hope that you are still interested in having the extension built in March.

Best regards,

Marcus Barker

49. According to the e-mail, what did Marcus Barker try to do in January?

    (A) Fix the server used in his office

    (B) Call Clifford Randall several times

    (C) Send Clifford Randall an estimate

    (D) Finish renovating an office

50. What is included with the e-mail?

    (A) An estimate

    (B) A contract

    (C) A letter of apology

    (D) A renovation schedule

51. What is Clifford Randall asked to do?

    (A) Wait for a phone call from Marcus Barker

    (B) Let Marcus Barker know if he agrees to the price

    (C) Verify that he has received both e-mails

    (D) Sign a contract by the end of the week

做完之後，在下方表格填入作答時間與答對題數。

第 1 回 ＿＿＿月＿＿＿日	第 2 回 ＿＿＿月＿＿＿日	第 3 回 ＿＿＿月＿＿＿日
答對題數 ＿＿＿題 時間 ＿＿＿分＿＿＿秒	答對題數 ＿＿＿題 時間 ＿＿＿分＿＿＿秒	答對題數 ＿＿＿題 時間 ＿＿＿分＿＿＿秒

翻譯及解析

49-51 題參考以下電子郵件。

收件人：Clifford Randall
寄件人：Marcus Barker
主旨：道歉
日期：2 月 18 日

親愛的 Randall 先生：

對於沒有早點通知您擴建一事，我很抱歉。我明白您自 3 週前開完 1 月會議以來，就一直等候我們消息。開完會之後，我們馬上就寄出電子郵件給您，但昨天收到您的訊息之後，我們才發現您沒收到。調查此事之後，發現我們公司在 1 月中到 2 月初進行整修，而造成伺服器發生問題，先前寄給您的郵件因而寄丟。先前一起寄丟的估價單，我也附在這封信件中。過目之後，請撥打 555-0942，通知我是否同意報價。確認價格之後，我會帶一份紙本合約拜訪您。我再次為這次的延誤致上歉意，也希望您仍有意在 3 月進行擴建。

Marcus Barker 敬啟

---

49. 根據電子郵件，Marcus Barker 在 1 月做了什麼？

(A) 修理辦公室的伺服器
(B) 打好幾次電話給 Clifford Randall
(C) 寄估價單給 Clifford Randall
(D) 辦公室整修完工

正確答案：C　　　選項對照

先找出人名，再根據題目關鍵字 January 尋找線索。這是 Marcus Barker 寄給 Clifford Randall 的電子郵件，第 3 行提到 our January meeting three weeks ago. We tried sending you an e-mail immediately after the meeting，可知 Marcus Barker 有試著寄電子郵件給 Clifford Randall。此外，從第 12 行的 Along with the message we tried sending you was a draft of the estimate...，可知他在那封電子郵件有附上草擬估價單，答案是 (C)。

50. 電子郵件中夾帶了什麼？

(A) 估價單   (B) 合約

(C) 道歉信   (D) 整修進度表

正確答案：A   選項對照

找出電子郵件所夾帶的內容。從第 12 行的 Along with the message we tried sending you was a draft of the estimate, which is attached to this message. 可知，沒寄出去的草擬估價單已經附加在電子郵件裡頭，答案是 (A)。

ⓘ 在電子郵件的文章中，只要看到 include、attach 或 enclose，就是與附加檔案有關的訊息。

---

51. Clifford Randall 被要求做什麼事？

(A) 等待 Marcus Barker 的電話

(B) 讓 Marcus Barker 知道是否同意報價

(C) 確認兩封電子郵件都收到

(D) 在本週簽定合約

正確答案：B   選項對照

這題問收件人 Clifford Randall 受託要做什麼事。寄件人在第 15 行提到 please call me at 555-0942 and let me know if you find the price agreeable，希望 Clifford Randall 致電通知是否接受該價格，答案是 (B)。

ⓘ 答題線索是 please，請求他人做事時，也會用到這個字。此外，請求事項通常會放在信件開頭或後半部，請仔細閱讀這兩個部分。

單字

- **apology** *(n.)* 道歉
  (v.) **apologize** 道歉
- **extension** *(n.)* 擴建；分機
- **immediately** *(adv.)* 立即
- **along with** 連同
- **draft** *(n.)* 草稿
- **estimate** *(n.)* 估價單
  (v.) **estimate** 估價；評估

- **agreeable** *(adj.)* 可接受的
- **once** *(conj.)* 一旦
- **settle on** 決定
- **contract** *(n.)* 合約
- **verify** *(v.)* 確認；證實

Jacksonville Port Restaurant's
100th Year

We are excited to invite our guests to join us for some very special times in celebration of the Jacksonville Port Restaurant's centennial anniversary from Wednesday, August 3 to Saturday, August 6. During this time, live music and other entertainment will be featured nightly in our main dining room as well as on our terrace overlooking the Jacksonville River and port.

Originally established as the port's pub in the late 1800s, the building evolved into one of Louisiana's finest and most celebrated dining establishments. Today, restaurant owner Guy Frederic is pleased to unveil the restaurant's upcoming schedule for its week of celebration.

On Wednesday, Chef Gregory Madden will hold a cooking demonstration from 5:00 P.M. before the Bankstring Band takes some of Louisiana's best blues to the stage. The band will perform inside every night while Clive Hanley serenades the outdoor terrace with jazz and his guitar. On Saturday, Pastry Chef Melanie Carter will show guests how to prepare a selection of the restaurant's signature desserts followed by a wine and champagne party to toast the establishment's birthday.

For details and reservations, contact the Jacksonville Port Restaurant at 555-2034.

52. What is the announcement mainly about?
    (A) A reopening
    (B) A review
    (C) A discount
    (D) An anniversary

53. What is scheduled for August 3?
    (A) A cooking show
    (B) A free buffet
    (C) A wine seminar
    (D) A champagne toast

54. What is indicated about the restaurant?
    (A) It is next to a lake.
    (B) It will have a one-week event.
    (C) It has recently reopened.
    (D) It has a seating area outside.

55. Who owns the Jacksonville Port Restaurant?
    (A) Melanie Carter
    (B) Gregory Madden
    (C) Clive Hanley
    (D) Guy Frederic

第 1 回 ＿＿月＿＿日	第 2 回 ＿＿月＿＿日	第 3 回 ＿＿月＿＿日
答對題數 ＿＿＿題 時間 ＿＿＿分＿＿＿秒	答對題數 ＿＿＿題 時間 ＿＿＿分＿＿＿秒	答對題數 ＿＿＿題 時間 ＿＿＿分＿＿＿秒

翻譯及解析

52-55 題參考以下公告。

傑克森威爾港餐廳一百歲了

傑克森威爾港餐廳很榮幸邀請各位參加在 8 月 3 日星期三到 8 月 6 日星期六所舉行的一百週年特別活動。這段期間，每晚在主餐廳與能俯瞰傑克森威爾河與港口的露天座位區，會有現場演奏與其他娛樂活動。

這棟建築物興建於 19 世紀末，原本是港口酒吧，後來進化成路易斯安那州最高級知名的餐廳之一。今日餐廳老闆 Guy Frederic 很榮幸為各位揭幕為期一週的慶祝活動。

星期三下午 5 點開始，主廚 Gregory Madden 將會示範烹飪表演，接著 Bankstring 樂團將會帶來路易斯安那州最棒的藍調演奏。樂團每晚將於室內演奏，同時 Clive Hanley 也會在戶外平台演奏吉他與爵士樂。週六甜點師 Melanie Carter 將會為各位準備本餐廳一系列的招牌甜點，接著舉行紅酒香檳派對，敬邀各位舉杯共襄盛舉。

活動詳情與預約，請致電傑克森威爾港餐廳：555-2034。

---

52. 此公告主要是關於什麼？

(A) 重新開幕

(B) 審核

(C) 折扣

(D) 週年慶

正確答案：D　　　　　　　　　　　　　　　　　文章主旨

從標題 Jacksonville Port Restaurant's 100th Year 以及第一段第 1 行的 We are excited to invite our guests to join us for some very special times in celebration of the Jacksonville Port Restaurant's centennial anniversary，可得知本文是開店紀念日的公告，答案是 (D)。

ⓘ centennial anniversary 是「100 週年」。cent 指「100」，century、percent 這兩個字也有出現這個字根。

53. 8月3日預計安排什麼？

(A) 烹飪表演

(B) 免費自助餐

(C) 品酒會

(D) 香檳慶祝會

正確答案：A 詢問細節

題目的 August 3 是解題關鍵字，請尋找與時間有關的資訊。第一段第 2 行的 celebration of the Jacksonville Port Restaurant's centennial anniversary from Wednesday, August 3，可得知這一天是星期三。此外，第三段第 1 行提到 On Wednesday, Chef Gregory Madden will hold a cooking demonstration，表示星期三會示範烹飪表演。答案是 (A)。

①本題的答題線索分散在不同地方，解題時需找出兩者的關聯性。

54. 關於餐廳，本文提到什麼？

(A) 開在湖邊。

(B) 將會舉行一週活動。

(C) 最近重新開幕。

(D) 室外有座位區。

正確答案：D 選項對照

這間餐廳有 terrace「露天座位」這項資訊，可從第一段第 7 行的 on our terrace 和第三段第 6 行的 the outdoor terrace 得知。由於露天座位是在室外，答案是 (D)。

55. 誰擁有傑克森威爾港餐廳？

(A) Melanie Carter

(B) Gregory Madden

(C) Clive Hanley

(D) Guy Frederic

正確答案：D 詢問細節

題目的 owns「擁有」是解題關鍵字。從第二段第 4 行的 restaurant owner Guy Frederic，可知這人是餐廳老闆，答案是 (D)。

單字

- centennial anniversary 一百週年
- entertainment *(n.)* 娛樂活動
- feature *(v.)* 以～為特色，主打
- nightly *(adj.)* 每夜的
- terrace *(n.)* 露天座位區，露天平台
- overlook *(v.)* 俯瞰
- originally *(adv.)* 原本
- establish *(v.)* 建立
- evolve *(v.)* 進化
- fine *(adj.)* 高級的
- celebrated *(adj.)* 有名的
- dining establishment 餐廳
- unveil *(v.)* 公開，揭開

- demonstration *(n.)* 示範，表演
  (v.) demonstrate 示範
- perform *(v.)* 表演
  (n.) performance 演奏
- serenade *(v.)* 演奏
- signature dessert 招牌甜點
- followed by 接著是，隨後是
- toast *(v.)/(n.)* 舉杯祝賀；慶祝會
- review *(n.)/(v.)* 審查
- schedule *(v.)/(n.)* 安排行程；行程（表）
- buffet *(n.)* 自助餐
- wine seminar 品酒會

This is a summary report for yesterday's board meeting regarding our Web site.

• COMPANY PROFILE

The page design is attractive and well laid out for customers to easily find information. Written both clearly and concisely, the company history includes all relevant information. The story tracing the company's past from its foundation to the present attracts interest and leaves a strong impression. Overall, we do not need to change this section.

• RECRUITMENT

Information on this page must stay current. There are four security positions still listed as open, even though they have already been filled. Also, the openings for the marketing manager positions, listed in the newspaper two weeks ago, have not been uploaded to the Web site. The communications department should be maintaining steady cooperation with personnel in promptly addressing issues such as these.

• CONTACT INFORMATION

Despite the idea being rejected in a board meeting last year, we now feel a customer feedback form needs to be added to this section. With the form, we will be able to know where our customers' needs lie in order to quickly respond to them. Once the form has been approved and is part of the site, all feedback will be sent directly to the customer service manager Shutaro Ishino (ishino@arlco.tex.com).

The communications department will look into the above issues, discuss them, and send Shutaro Ishino and me a plan for the site's next redesign. We all know that for many of our customers, the Web site is where they first get impressions about us, and with this in mind, a thoroughly considered plan is needed by the end of next week.

Emilio Hernandez
Arlco Texas Ltd.
General Affairs

56. What is the purpose of the report?
    (A) To propose a new Web site plan
    (B) To reject modifications to a Web site
    (C) To report results from a meeting
    (D) To request a budget for Web site redesign

57. According to the report, what information is accurate on the Web site?
    (A) The corporate history
    (B) The sales figures
    (C) The job openings
    (D) The contact number

58. What can be inferred about the customer feedback form?
    (A) It will lower the workload of the sales division.
    (B) It has been added to the company's Web site.
    (C) It will be modified by the customer service manager.
    (D) It was discussed in a board meeting last year.

59. In the report, what position is mentioned as still being open?

(A) Security engineer

(B) Customer service representative

(C) Marketing manager

(D) Web site designer

60. What will happen by the end of next week?

(A) A plan will be drafted.

(B) A Web site will be launched.

(C) A board meeting will take place.

(D) A form will be added.

做完之後，在下方表格填入作答時間與答對題數。

第 1 回 ＿＿月＿＿日	第 2 回 ＿＿月＿＿日	第 3 回 ＿＿月＿＿日
答對題數 ＿＿題 時間 ＿＿分＿＿秒	答對題數 ＿＿題 時間 ＿＿分＿＿秒	答對題數 ＿＿題 時間 ＿＿分＿＿秒

翻譯及解析

以下是昨日董事會上與網站相關的簡報。

• 公司簡介

此處網頁設計引人注目，版面編排讓訪客可輕易找到資訊。公司歷史寫得清楚簡潔，含括所有相關資訊。公司故事回顧公司從草創到如今規模，會引起興趣且留下深刻印象。整體而言，這一塊不需更動。

• 員工招聘

本頁資訊請務必隨時更新。有 4 個保安職缺仍開放，但是這些職缺已經找到人了。此外，兩週前刊登在報紙上的行銷經理職缺，尚未上傳到這裡。通訊部與人事部應保持穩定合作，迅速因應這類問題。

• 聯絡資訊

儘管這個建議在去年董事會上被否決，不過我們現在認為，這一區塊有必要加入客戶意見表。有了這個表單，我們才能知道客戶真正需求，進而快速因應。一旦表單通過，成為此網站一部分，所有回饋意見就會直接寄到客服經理 Shutaro Ishino 的電子信箱（ishino@arlco.tex.com）。

通訊部要針對以上問題進行調查並討論，並寄送下一波網站修改計畫給 Shutaro Ishino 跟我。我們都知道，對多數顧客而言，網站是他們獲得公司第一印象的地方，請將這點謹記在心，在下週五之前提交妥善計畫。

Emilio Hernandez
行政部
德州 Arlco 股份有限公司

56. 此報告的目的為何？

(A) 提出新的網站計畫
(B) 拒絕修改網站一事
(C) 報告會議結果
(D) 請求網站重新設計的預算

正確答案：C　　　　　　　　　　　　　　　　　　**文章目的**

開頭句提到 This is a summary report for yesterday's board meeting regarding our Web site.，並在接下來的句子說明，此概要是 yesterday's board meeting 所討論的內容，答案是 (C)。

57. 根據報告，網站上何種資訊正確？

(A) 企業歷史

(B) 銷售數字

(C) 職缺

(D) 聯絡電話

正確答案：**A** 　　　　　　　　　　　　　　　　　　 `詢問細節`

題目的 accurate「正確的」是解題關鍵字。從 Company Profile「公司簡介」第 3 行的 the company history includes all relevant information，以及第 7 行的 Overall, we do not need to change this section.，可推斷 (A) The corporate history 相關的資訊才是正確的。(B) Sales figures「銷售數字」與 (D) Contact numbers「聯絡電話」在文中沒有提及，因此不是答案。

58. 關於客戶意見表，從本文可推論出什麼？

(A) 將會減輕銷售部門工作量。

(B) 已經加入公司網站中。

(C) 將會由客服經理作修改。

(D) 去年在董事會已經討論過。

正確答案：**D** 　　　　　　　　　　　　　　　　　　 `推論題`

這題要選出可從文中推論出來的選項。關鍵字 the customer feedback form「客戶意見表」出現在 Contact Information「聯絡資訊」段落中，從第 1 行的 Despite the idea being rejected in a board meeting last year 可推斷，去年董事會有討論過這項議題。答案是 (D)。

ⓘ 題目若出現 infer（推測）、imply（暗示）或 suggest（暗示）等字，就是推論題，需從文中推敲出答案。

59. 報告中哪個職位仍有開缺？

(A) 安全工程師

(B) 客服人員

(C) 行銷經理

(D) 網站設計師

正確答案：C　　　　　　　　　　　　　　　　詢問細節

題目和 position「職位」有關，因此可從 Recruitment「招募員工」下方的內文尋找線索。第 4 行提到 the openings for the marketing manager positions, listed in the newspaper two weeks ago, have not been uploaded to the Web site.，答案是 (C)。

....

60. 下週五之前會發生什麼事？

(A) 會擬好一份計畫。

(B) 啟用網站。

(C) 召開董事會會議。

(D) 新增一個表單。

正確答案：A　　　　　　　　　　　　　　　　詢問細節

出現在報告最後一段的 by the end of next week「下週以前」是關鍵字，這段提到 a thoroughly considered plan is needed by the end of next week，表示下週前會擬定計畫，答案是 (A)。

ⓘ draft 當名詞時，有「原稿」、「草案」之意，當動詞則有「起草（文件或計畫）」的意思，這裡以被動式 be drafted 表達。

單字

- board meeting 董事會會議
- profile (n.) 簡介
- concisely (adv.) 簡明扼要地
- relevant (adj.) 相關的
- trace (v.) 追溯，查出
- foundation (n.) 創立
  (v.) found 創立
- the present 現在，目前
- impression (n.) 印象
  (v.) impress 使～印象深刻
- recruitment (n.) 招募
  (v.) recruit 招募
- stay (v.) 維持某種狀態（+ adj.）
- opening (n.) 職缺
  (adj.) open 開缺的
- upload (v.) 上傳
- communications department
  傳訊部門
- maintain (v.) 維持
- steady (adj.) 穩定的
- cooperation (n.) 合作
- promptly (adv.) 迅速地

- address (v.) 處理（問題）
- despite (prep.) 儘管（表轉折語氣）
- reject (v.) 否決
- feedback (n.) 回饋
- respond (v.) 回應
- approve (v.) 認可，准許
- redesign (n.) 設計變更
- in mind 記住
- thoroughly (adv.) 徹底地
- consider (v.) 考量
- propose (v.) 提出
- modification (n.) 修正
  (v.) modify 修正
- budget (n.) 預算
- accurate (adj.) 準確的
- lower (v.) 減低
- workload (n.) 工作量
- customer service representative
  客服人員
- draft (v.)/(n.) 起草；草案
- launch (v.) 啟用；推出，發表

FISH TAIL FREDDY'S OCEAN GRILL

∾ *Crab Cakes Deluxe* $12.99
Two blue crab cakes with our special blend of herbs
and spices served with a caper, carrot, and mustard sauce

∾ *Prince Edward Mussels* $9.99
One pound of mussels sautéed in white wine, garlic,
and capers, and served with barbecued tomatoes

∾ *Smoked Salmon Penne* $8.99
Smoked salmon on a bed of penne, served with a roast
garlic, brandy, tomato, and herb sauce

∾ *Surf and Turf* $16.99
Tender medallions of beef alongside succulent Maine
lobster, with fresh vegetables and garlic sauce

All items are complemented with a choice of
sautéed vegetables or steamed broccoli and
cauliflower, and your choice of jasmine rice,
brown rice, garlic mashed potatoes, baked
potato, or French fries.

OUR TASTY SPRING SPECIALS

❧ *Grilled Quesadillas* $10.69

Flour tortillas, cheddar cheese, scallions, chilies,
and six types of peppers served with chicken and shrimp

❧ *Cajun Calamari Salad* $6.89

Cajun coated calamari, tomatoes, and julienne carrots
served with Dijon vinaigrette

❧ *Grilled Grouper* $14.69

Served Naples style with a purée of black olives,
capers, garlic, parsley, and cherry tomatoes

❧ *Twin Lobster Tails* $16.99

Enjoy Maine's finest—Twin lobster tails brushed lightly
with garlic, barbecued, and served with butter sauce

- For parties of eight or more, a 15% gratuity
  will be added to the bill.

- Please ask your waiter about Fish Tail Freddy's daily
  specials and famous cocktails.

- Check out our performance, The Mermaid
  Dance (every Saturday evening from 8:00).

FISH TAIL FREDDY'S
THE NEW HOT SPOT TO DINE

A Maine original, Fish Tail Freddy's Ocean Grill is the place to dine for great food and a spectacular view of the coast. With a unique seafood menu and its ocean-themed décor, Freddy's owner and chef Fred McCabe boasts of using only the freshest products, creating a fabulous blend of seafood and foreign dishes with a Maine flare.

With over 100 items on the menu, choosing my supper was not easy, but thanks to Freddy's first-rate staff, I had the opportunity to sample several of Freddy's favorites. From stuffed crab Rangoon, brandy-basted swordfish, and East Coast crab cakes to salmon steak and Freddy's Bucket of Shrimp, this restaurant certainly has something for everyone. I recommend the Cajun calamari salad for starters followed by the spicy grilled trout. Or for those of you that like it really hot, try the jalapeño shrimp—too hot for me but a popular choice at Freddy's according to staff.

And not only are some dishes on the menu hot. I had the opportunity to see the show, featuring four dancers dressed in mermaid costumes and doing all sorts of incredible acrobatics on Freddy's stage.

The prices are reasonable, the atmosphere comfortable, and it's open every day for lunch and dinner, but if you want to go to Freddy's, make sure to make a reservation first. The place is packed most nights and at lunchtime on weekends, and finding a parking spot is not easy. But once the car is parked, get ready for some great food at a fantastic restaurant.

61. What night did the reviewer go to the restaurant?

(A) Tuesday

(B) Friday

(C) Saturday

(D) Sunday

62. What is NOT served for free with Cajun Calamari Salad?

(A) Dijon vinaigrette

(B) Scrambled eggs

(C) Baked potato

(D) Sautéed vegetables

63. In the review, the word "packed" in paragraph 4, line 8, is closest in meaning to

(A) unavailable

(B) crowded

(C) wrapped

(D) engaged

64. How did the reviewer describe the restaurant staff?

    (A) Fast
    (B) Famous
    (C) Excellent
    (D) Unique

65. What was the reviewer NOT satisfied with at the restaurant?

    (A) The scenery
    (B) The prices
    (C) The dance show
    (D) The hot food

做完之後，在下方表格填入作答時間與答對題數。

第 1 回 ＿＿＿月＿＿＿日	第 2 回 ＿＿＿月＿＿＿日	第 3 回 ＿＿＿月＿＿＿日
答對題數 ＿＿＿題 時間 ＿＿＿分＿＿＿秒	答對題數 ＿＿＿題 時間 ＿＿＿分＿＿＿秒	答對題數 ＿＿＿題 時間 ＿＿＿分＿＿＿秒

翻譯及解析

魚尾 FREDDY 海鮮燒烤 春季美味特選

- **豪華蟹肉餅**   12.99 元
  兩塊花蟹肉餅加上特製香草香料，佐酸豆、紅蘿蔔與芥末醬

- **愛德華王子淡菜**   9.99 元
  一磅淡菜以白酒、大蒜及酸豆拌炒，佐烤番茄

- **燻鮭魚通心粉**   8.99 元
  一大盤通心粉加上煙燻鮭魚，佐烤大蒜、白蘭地、番茄與香草醬

- **海陸雙拼**   16.99 元
  無骨軟嫩牛排加上來自緬因州的多汁龍蝦，搭配新鮮蔬菜與香草醬

- **墨西哥起司烤餅**   10.69 元
  全麵粉墨西哥薄餅、切達起司、青蔥、辣椒，與 6 種胡椒搭配雞肉與海蝦

- **香辣烏賊圈沙拉**   6.89 元
  烏賊裹上卡津香料、番茄與胡蘿蔔絲，搭配第戎油醋醬

- **烤石斑魚**   14.69 元
  以拿坡里風料理，加入純黑橄欖、酸豆、大蒜、荷蘭芹與小番茄

- **雙尾龍蝦**   16.99 元
  享受來自緬因州最高級的雙尾龍蝦，以烤大蒜輕刷再上架烘烤，搭配奶油醬使用

> 所有料理皆配上炒蔬菜或蒸花椰菜，您可以選擇搭配泰國香米、糙米、大蒜馬鈴薯泥、烤馬鈴薯或薯條。

- 8 人以上團體來賓，酌收 15% 服務費。
- 每日特餐與知名雞尾酒，請洽詢服務生。
- 看看我們的表演團體，人魚舞團（每週六晚上 8 點開始）。

魚尾 FREDDY
最新人氣美食

緬因州道地的魚尾 Freddy 海鮮燒烤，一向是品嚐美食、觀賞美麗海景的好地方。擁有獨一無二的海鮮料理與海洋風裝潢，Freddy 店長兼主廚 Fred McCabe 驕傲地說，自家只使用最新鮮海產，以緬因州風味混搭出令人驚艷的海鮮與異國餐點。

菜單上超過一百道餐點，要挑出想吃的還真不簡單。不過，感謝 Freddy 一流的服務人員，我有機會試吃好幾道 Freddy 顧客最愛料理。從蟹角、白蘭地劍魚、美國東岸蟹肉餅、鮭魚排，到 Freddy 招牌蝦籃，這家餐廳確實能滿足每個人的味蕾。我的推薦吃法如下：香辣烏賊圈沙拉作為開胃菜，接著品嚐辣烤鱒魚。如果你是無辣不歡的人，試試看墨西哥蝦——這道菜對我來說太辣，不過根據店內服務人員，這道是人氣料理。

這裡不光只有餐點辣而已。我有機會一賞 Freddy 舞台上的人魚秀，特色是 4 位身穿美人魚裝的舞者，演出各種令人歎為觀止的特技表演。

這裡的價位合理，氣氛舒適，全年供應午晚餐，如果你想來 Freddy 用餐，務必提前預約。這裡的晚間時段與平日午餐時段經常客滿，停車位一位難求。不過，只要你有機會停好車，就可以準備大啖一頓。

61. 評論者在哪天晚上光顧餐廳？

(A) 星期二
(B) 星期五
(C) 星期六
(D) 星期日

正確答案：C

整合資訊

題目問評論撰寫者（reviewer）在星期幾造訪店家，可在評論裡找答案。不過評論中沒有標註造訪日期，而答案線索就在第三段第 3 行的 I had the opportunity to see the show, featuring four dancers dressed in mermaid costumes...，這段敘述呼應了菜單最後一行的 Check out our performance, The Mermaid Dance (every Saturday evening from 8:00).。可知人魚表演是在星期六，答案是 (C)。

ⓘ 只要找出菜單與評論之間的關聯性，就可以順利解題。在雙篇閱讀題，5 題裡就會有 1 到 2 題是需要參照兩篇文章的題目，請特別留意。

62. 以下何種食物沒有跟香辣烏賊圈沙拉一起上？

(A) 第戎油醋醬

(B) 炒蛋

(C) 烤馬鈴薯

(D) 炒蔬菜

正確答案：**B**

詢問細節 ＋ NOT 題

用 Cajun Calamari Salad 這個關鍵字來對照菜單內容的話，會發現這道菜的說明裡寫到 served with Dijon vinaigrette。此外，菜單左下角灰底處也提到 All items are complemented with a choice of sautéed vegetables... baked potato...，沒有提到 Scrambled eggs，答案是 (B)。

ⓘ 本文雖然出現許多陌生的飲食名詞，但不影響作答，畢竟多益不會考「什麼是 Quesadillas？」這種題目。只要沉穩作答，仔細對照選項跟內文，就能輕鬆解題。

---

63. 評論中第四段第 8 行的 packed 一字，意思最接近

(A) unavailable「沒有供應的」

(B) crowded「擁擠的」

(C) wrapped「包裝好的」

(D) engaged「訂婚的」

正確答案：**B**

同義字題

評論第四段第 8 行裡，packed 這個字出現在 The place is packed most nights and at lunchtime on weekends 這個句子裡，表「擁擠」之意，與 (B) crowded 的意思相同。

ⓘpacked 也指「打包好的」。切記，同義字題是要找出「符合上下文」的字。

64. 評論家如何敘述餐廳工作人員？

(A) 動作快速的

(B) 有名的

(C) 優秀的

(D) 獨一無二的

正確答案：**C**

尋找細節

找出有關店員的敘述。第二段第 3 行提到了 thanks to Freddy's first-rate staff，答案是 (C)。

ⓘ first-rate「一流的」等於 excellent「優秀的」，如果不曉得就無法答題。單字實力定生死就是這麼一回事。

65. 評論家不滿意餐廳哪一點？

(A) 景色

(B) 價位

(C) 舞蹈表演

(D) 辣食

正確答案：**D**

NOT ＋推論題

題目詢問評論者對什麼不滿，因此要看第 2 篇評論找答案。第二段倒數第 5 行提到，try the jalapeño shrimp—too hot for me but a popular choice at Freddy's according to staff.，可知評論者覺得 jalapeño shrimp 太辣了，因此答案可說是 (D) The hot food。

ⓘ 文中並沒有用 I wasn't satisfied with... 這種明確的敘述，需要自己推敲出 too hot for me 這句話暗示了「因為太辣所以不喜歡」。

單字

- grill *(n.)/(v.)* 燒烤
- cake *(n.)* 肉餅；蛋糕
- blend of ～的混搭
- herb *(n.)* 香草
- spice *(n.)* 調味料
- serve *(v.)* 供應（餐點）
- caper *(n.)* 酸豆
- mussel *(n.)* 淡菜（一種貝類）
- mustard *(n.)* 芥末
- sauté *(v.)* 煎
- medallion *(n.)* 軟嫩圓形肉片
- alongside *(prep.)* 與～一起
- succulent *(adj.)* 多汁的
- complement *(v.)* 搭配，補足
- steam *(v.)* 蒸
- broccoli *(n.)* 綠花椰菜
- cauliflower *(n.)* 白花椰菜
- jasmine rice 泰國香米
- quesadilla *(n.)* 墨西哥起司餡餅
- tortilla *(n.)* 墨西哥薄餅
- scallion *(n.)* 青蔥
- shrimp *(n.)* 蝦
- calamari *(n.)* 花枝
- julienne *(adj.)* 切絲的
- vinaigrette *(n.)* 油醋醬
- cherry tomato 小番茄
- gratuity *(n.)* 小費（正式用法）
- daily special 本日特餐

- mermaid *(n.)* 美人魚
- hot spot 人氣景點
- dine *(v.)* 用餐
- spectacular *(adj.)* 令人驚艷的；壯觀的
- décor *(n.)* 內裝
- boast of 以～自豪
- fabulous *(adj.)* 出色的
- flare *(n.)* 風味
- first-rate *(adj.)* 一流的
- opportunity *(n.)* 機會
- sample *(v.)/(n.)* 試吃；試吃品，試用品
- stuffed *(adj.)* 塞滿的
- basted *(adj.)* 抹上油脂的
- has something for everyone
  能滿足每個人的
- swordfish *(n.)* 劍魚
- starter *(n.)* 前菜
- trout *(n.)* 鱒魚
- costume *(n.)* 服裝
- acrobatics *(n.)* 雜技
- atmosphere *(n.)* 氣氛
- packed *(adj.)* 客滿的，擁擠的
- unavailable *(adj.)* 無法取得的；沒空的
- crowded *(adj.)* 擁擠的
- wrapped *(adj.)* 包起來的
- engaged *(adj.)*
  已預約的；忙線中；有人使用的

NOTE

To: Kumiko Remy

From: Natalie Poliskova

Subject: The Vienna Conference

Date: April 27

Dear Kumiko:

Six months have passed since I left HERC Corp.,
but it feels as though I just left yesterday.
How is everything going there in the research
department? I hope all is well. As for me, I am
used to my new work environment at Etcher
Pharmaceuticals. The people I work with are very
good at what they do, and I have learned a lot
here.

I assume you will again be attending the medical
conference in Vienna this June. I have a meeting
to attend in Berlin on June 1 but will fly from
there to Austria on June 2 for the conference's
second day. I have not looked at the schedule
yet but expect HERC will be doing a lecture

again this year on malaria research. Will William
Herbert or Aziza Rashid be speaking? If the
HERC lecture is not on the first, I would be very
happy to meet you beforehand for coffee or tea.
Afterward, we could go to the lecture together.

I look forward to hearing from you soon.

Natalie Poliskova

• The Vienna Conference on Malaria

ROOM	DESCRIPTION
Committee Room D (SID Centre)	Malaria & Mosquitoes: Facing the challenges with scientific research
Committee Room B (SID Centre)	Feasibility of training traditional healers to treat malaria cases in tribal areas of northern India
Hall A (NAC Complex)	A novel LVR method for rapid diagnosis of the malaria parasite
Committee Room C (SID Centre)	New findings in malaria resistance in South America
Committee Room B (SID Centre)	Closing Address: The future of malaria treatment
Banquet Hall (NAC Complex)	The Herbert Feldman Dinner

Schedule for June 2

TIME	SPEAKER
10:00–12:00	Carmen W. Mendis, Switzerland
12:30–14:00	Savaan Malhotra, India
14:10–15:30	Kenichi Sakai, Japan
15:40–16:30	William Herbert, England
16:40–17:30	P. K. Joshi, India
19:00–21:30	Various

All lectures require pre-registration except for the closing address, which is open to the public. For the dinner, reservations are required and can be made on the day, before 11:00 A.M.

66. Who is going to talk about a way to quickly diagnose malaria?

    (A) Aziza Rashid

    (B) Savaan Malhotra

    (C) Kenichi Sakai

    (D) William Herbert

67. Who is going to give a lecture not requiring registration?

    (A) Carmen W. Mendis

    (B) Kumiko Remy

    (C) William Herbert

    (D) P. K. Joshi

68. What is NOT mentioned about Natalie Poliskova?

    (A) She will speak at the conference.

    (B) She is flying from Berlin on June 2.

    (C) She is accustomed to her new job.

    (D) She used to work for HERC Corp.

69. In the e-mail, the word "assume" in paragraph 2, line 1, is closest in meaning to
(A) strive
(B) favor
(C) guess
(D) question

70. Where will Natalie Poliskova and Kumiko Remy attend a lecture together?
(A) In Hall A
(B) In Committee Room B
(C) In Committee Room C
(D) In Committee Room D

第1回 ____月____日	第2回 ____月____日	第3回 ____月____日
答對題數 ____題 時間 ____分____秒	答對題數 ____題 時間 ____分____秒	答對題數 ____題 時間 ____分____秒

翻譯及解析

收件人：Kumiko Remy

寄件人：Natalie Poliskova

主旨：維也納研討會

日期：4 月 27 日

親愛的 Kumiko：

我離開 HERC 公司也有半年了，不過感覺好像昨天才離開。

研究部門最近可好？希望你們一切順利。我已經適應 Etcher 製藥公司的工作環境。跟我一起共事的人都很專業，我在這裡學到很多。

我想，你今年也會參加 6 月在維也納舉行的醫學研討會。我 6 月 1 日會去柏林參加會議，不過我 6 月 2 日會直接飛到奧地利，參加第二天的研討會。我還沒看過研討會日程，不過我預計 HERC 今年應該會再次針對瘧疾發表演講。講者會是 William Herbert 還是 Aziza Rashid？如果 HERC 的演講不是在第一天，我希望我們能先一起喝咖啡或茶，接著一起去聽演講。期待很快收到你的回音。

Natalie Poliskova

● 維也納瘧疾研討會 　　　　　　　　　　　　　　　　　　　　　　　6 月 2 日行程

演講廳	説明	時段	講者
會議室 D（SID 中心）	瘧疾與蚊子：以科學研究面對挑戰	10:00–12:00	Carmen W. Mendis，瑞士
會議室 B（SID 中心）	培訓北印度部落傳統治療師處理瘧疾病患之可行性	12:30–14:00	Savaan Malhotra，印度
A 廳（NAC 綜合大樓）	快速診斷瘧原蟲的新型 LVR 法	14:10–15:30	Kenichi Sakai，日本
會議室 C（SID 中心）	南美洲瘧疾抗藥性的新發現	15:40–16:30	William Herbert，英國
會議室 B（SID 中心）	閉幕演説：瘧疾防治的未來	16:40–17:30	P. K. Joshi，印度
宴會廳（NAC 綜合大樓）	赫伯費耳德曼餐廳	19:00–21:30	多位

除閉幕演説之外，其餘講座皆需事先報名。一般民眾皆可報名。晚宴需事先預約，當天早上 11 點前可接受預約。

66. 誰將主講快速診斷瘧疾的方法？

(A) Aziza Rashid

(B) Savaan Malhotra

(C) Kenichi Sakai

(D) William Herbert

正確答案：C　　　　　　　　　　　　　　　　　　**詢問細節**

題目的 quickly diagnose malaria「快速診斷瘧疾」是解題關鍵字，呼應議程表第 3 項的 rapid diagnosis of the malaria parasite。從 Speaker「講者」一欄的資訊可知，講座講者是 (C) Kenichi Sakai。

ⓘ diagnose「診斷」是動詞，diagnosis 則是名詞。另外，quickly（副詞）也呼應 rapid（形容詞）。議程表的主題看似艱澀，但這類表格資訊題很簡單，只要掌握幾個關鍵字，就能找出答案。

67. 誰的演說不需事先報名？

(A) Carmen W. Mendis

(B) Kumiko Remy

(C) William Herbert

(D) P. K. Joshi

正確答案：D　　　　　　　　　　　　　　　　　　**NOT + 整合資訊**

這題要選出不需報名的講座講者。議程表下方說明提到 All lectures require pre-registration except for the closing address, which is open to the public.，可知 the closing address「閉幕演講」不需事前報名。而 the closing address 就是議程上的第 5 個講座，講者是 (D) P. K. Joshi。

ⓘ 作答這題有 2 個步驟，首先要看完表格下方的注意事項，再用 the closing address 這個線索回頭對照本文。

68. 關於 Natalie Poliskova，何者敘述沒有提及？

(A) 她會在研討會上演說。

(B) 她在 6 月 2 日從柏林搭機出發。

(C) 她已經適應新工作。

(D) 她在 HERC 工作過。

正確答案：A　　　　　　　　　　　　　　　　　　NOT 題

題目詢問 Natalie Poliskova 的相關資訊，可在電子郵件中尋找答案。(B) She is flying from Berlin on June 2. 呼應第二段第 2 行 I have a meeting to attend in Berlin on June 1 but will fly from there to Austria on June 2 for the conference's second day.；(C) She is accustomed to her new job. 呼應第一段第 4 行的 I am used to my new work environment at Etcher Pharmaceuticals.，這裡的 accustomed to「適應～」對應到文中的 be used to「習慣～」。(D) She used to work for HERC Corp. 則呼應第一段第 1 行的 Six months have passed since I left HERC Corp.。只有 (A) She will speak at the conference. 未被提及，因此是答案。

69. 電子郵件第二段第 1 行的 assume，意思最接近

(A) strive「奮鬥」

(B) favor「喜好」

(C) guess「猜測」

(D) question「質疑」

正確答案：C　　　　　　　　　　　　　　　　　　同義字題

電子郵件第二段第 1 行的 assume 用在「I assume you will again be attending the medical conference in Vienna this June.」這個句子裡，最接近意思的是 (C) guess。

ⓘ assume 除了當「猜想」，在 assume responsibility「承擔責任」這組片語裡，則與 accept、take 同義。

70. Natalie Poliskova 跟 Kumiko Remy 會在哪裡聽講座？

(A) A 廳

(B) 會議室 B

(C) 會議室 C

(D) 會議室 D

正確答案：C

Natalie Poliskova 在電子郵件裡詢問 Kumiko Remy: Will William Herbert or Aziza Rashid be speaking?（第二段第 7 行），可看出 William Herbert 和 Aziza Rashid 都隸屬 HERC。接著 Natalie Poliskova 邀請對方：I would be very happy to meet you beforehand for coffee or tea. Afterward, we could go to the lecture together.（第二段第 9 行），暗示兩人要一起參加的是 William Herbert 或 Aziza Rashid 主講的講座。而議程表的第 4 項，載明 William Herbert 的講座是在 Committee Room C (SID Centre) 舉行，答案是 (C)。

① 問題與 Natalie Poliskova 和 Kumiko Remy 有關，因此要先看電子郵件內文，而選項提到演講地點，因此也須參考議程表，是典型的雙篇閱讀題。須找出電子郵件與議程表的資訊關聯性，建議循「因為 A 所以 B，因為 B 所以 C」的邏輯順序解題。

單字

- conference *(n.)* 研討會
- as though 似乎
- research *(n.)* 研究
- be used to + Ving/N 習慣～
- assume *(v.)* 以為，猜想
- medical *(adj.)* 醫學的
- beforehand *(adv.)* 事先
- afterward *(adv.)* 之後
- face *(v.)* 面對
- scientific *(adj.)* 科學的
- feasibility *(n.)* 可行性
- healer *(n.)* 治療者
- tribal *(adj.)* 部落的
- novel *(adj.)* 新式的

- diagnosis *(n.)* 診斷
- *(v.)* diagnose 診斷
- parasite *(n.)* 寄生蟲
- resistance *(n.)* 抵抗力
- closing address 閉幕演說
- treatment *(n.)* 治療
- pre-registration *(n.)* 事前報名
- except for 除～以外（排除後者）
- lecture *(n.)/(v.)* 演講；發表演講
- be accustomed to + Ving/N 習慣～，適應～
- favor *(v.)* 偏好
- question *(v.)/(n.)* 疑問，質疑；問題

很重要！提升成績更需要健康管理

.... TEX 加藤

在健康管理方面，最重要的就是考前一天一定要睡飽。千萬不要熬夜唸書，確保自己有充足的睡眠。

我也曾經有過睡眠不足的經驗，結果隔天在腦袋一片空白的情況下去考試，這樣是不會有好成績的。

另外，考試當天不要睡到最後一刻才起床，可以提早起床，做聽力與閱讀練習做為暖身，讓大腦切換到英文模式。

另外，搭捷運或公車前往考場途中，也可以好好利用本書複習。

接著，用 54 分鐘 游完全程吧！

We have entered into a license agreement with Pinnacle Press, owner of the rights to the hit comic book *Angel Quest*. We are now planning to design and develop products featuring characters in the comic book. Currently, it is very popular among children between six and eleven years old, so our product line-up will target this age group and include school stationery, clothes, food packaging, and toys. An animated TV series as well as a movie version of *Angel Quest* will be released next year, at which time our products will be on the market. This means that there is a lot of work to be done over the next several months to bring product concept to form. There will be plenty of overtime available, so if you are interested in taking on extra hours, please let your supervisor know. Let's work together to make this project a big success!

1. **What is *Angel Quest*?**

   (A) An animated TV series

   (B) A comic book

   (C) A movie

   (D) A child's toy

2. **If employees want to do overtime, what should they do?**

   (A) Tell a supervisor

   (B) Fill out an application

   (C) Speak with the owner

   (D) Consult with coworkers

做完之後，在下方表格填入作答時間與答對題數。

第 1 回 ＿＿月＿＿日	第 2 回 ＿＿月＿＿日	第 3 回 ＿＿月＿＿日
答對題數 ＿＿題 時間 ＿＿分＿＿秒	答對題數 ＿＿題 時間 ＿＿分＿＿秒	答對題數 ＿＿題 時間 ＿＿分＿＿秒

翻譯及解析

1-2 題參考以下公告。

我們已經向擁有暢銷漫畫《天使任務》版權的 Pinnacle 出版社取得授權。我們打算設計並開發該漫畫角色的周邊商品。目前這部作品在 6-11 歲的孩童中相當有人氣，所以我們的產品線，包括文具、衣服、食品包裝到玩具，將鎖定在這個年齡層。

《天使任務》的電視卡通與電影也會在明年推出，到時我們的商品也會上市。這表示接下來幾個月，為了讓商品概念成形，我們有很多工作要做。到時會有大量的加班需求，有加班意願的同仁請向各自主管報告。我們一起努力，讓這個提案圓滿成功吧。

1. 《天使任務》是什麼？

(A) 電視動畫

(B) 漫畫

(C) 電影

(D) 兒童玩具

正確答案：B 　　　　　　　　　　　　　　**詢問細節**

Angel Quest 是解題關鍵字。從第 2 行提到的 the hit comic book *Angel Quest* 可知這是漫畫書名，答案為 (B)。

2. 如果員工想加班，他們該怎麼做？

(A) 告訴主管

(B) 填寫表格

(C) 跟老闆談

(D) 跟同事商量

正確答案：A 　　　　　　　　　　　　　　**詢問細節**

在本文搜尋關於 overtime「加班」的資訊。倒數第 2 行 There will be plenty of overtime available, so if you are interested in taking on extra hours, please let your supervisor know.，當中的 let your supervisor know 就是線索。因此答案是換句話說的 (A) Tell a supervisor。這種換句話說的題型經常出現在 Part 7，需留意。

單字

- enter into 簽訂（合約）
- license agreement 授權合約
- hit (n.) 大受歡迎的東西
- character (n.) 角色
- target (v.)/(n.) 鎖定；目標
- stationery (n.) 文具
- animated (adj.) 動畫的
- TV series 連續劇

- on the market 上市
- concept (n.) 概念
- plenty of 大量的
- overtime (adv.)/(n.) 加班
- supervisor (n.) 上司
  (v.) supervise 監督
- application (n.) 申請（表）
- consult (v.) 諮詢，請教

It has been 30 years since Frederick Hobbs bought a small piece of land and an old house in the middle of nowhere. Back then, the property cost a mere 11 thousand pounds, a tenth of what it is worth today. And the closest city, still with a population under 20 thousand, was 38 miles away. Even though Hobbs assured his friends he would turn the house into a successful business, in a recent interview for *Maxwell Magazine* he jokingly recalled many of them thinking he had gone mad. Hobbs, however, was not mad at all. Within a year he turned the rundown house into a 17-room inn. Naming it Grassy Meadows and advertising it in a magazine for outdoors enthusiasts, the inn soon became a popular spot for Londoners wanting a break from the city's fast pace without having to travel too far. These days, even though the road to the inn from the nearest town Carnesville has not been paved, the now 26-room inn is nearly always fully booked for several months in advance, proving that with an idea and enthusiasm, a business can become successful anywhere.

3. **What did Frederick Hobbs do first after buying the land?**

   (A) Remodeled the house

   (B) Placed an ad in a magazine

   (C) Asked for donations from his friends

   (D) Paved a road to the inn

4. **What can be inferred about Grassy Meadows?**

   (A) It is now connected with Carnesville by a paved road.

   (B) It is not far from London.

   (C) It is popular among people living in rural areas.

   (D) It has been operating for more than 30 years.

做完之後，在下方表格填入作答時間與答對題數。

第 **1** 回 ＿＿＿月＿＿＿日	第 **2** 回 ＿＿＿月＿＿＿日	第 **3** 回 ＿＿＿月＿＿＿日
答對題數 ＿＿＿題 時間 ＿＿＿分＿＿＿秒	答對題數 ＿＿＿題 時間 ＿＿＿分＿＿＿秒	答對題數 ＿＿＿題 時間 ＿＿＿分＿＿＿秒

3-4 題參考以下報導。

---

30 年前，Frederick Hobbs 在這片荒蕪之地買下一小塊土地與一間老屋，當時他只花了一萬一千英磅，是如今價格的十分之一。鄰近城市的人口不到兩萬人，距離這裡也有 38 英里之遙。即使如此，Hobbs 還是向好友保證，他會把這棟房子變成搖錢樹。接受 Maxwell 雜誌訪談時，他開玩笑地說，當時很多人說他瘋了。然而，Hobbs 根本沒瘋。他在一年之內，將這棟破舊老屋變成擁有 17 間客房的旅館，取名為綠地旅館，並且在戶外活動愛好者會看的雜誌上刊登廣告。對於想遠離快速步調的城市，但又不想出遠門旅行的倫敦人而言，這間旅館很快成為熱門景點。即使從最近的卡尼斯村前往旅館的道路尚未舖設，但如今已擁有 26 間客房的這間旅館依然預約滿檔，要提早好幾個月預約。這證明只要有想法與熱情，不管在何處都能成就事業。

---

3. Frederick Hobbs 買下土地後，做的第一件事是什麼？

(A) 改建房子 　　　　　　　　　(B) 在雜誌上刊登廣告

(C) 向好友要錢 　　　　　　　　(D) 舖設通往旅舍的路

正確答案：A　　　　　　　　　　　　　　　　　　　　選項對照

Hobbs 買下土地後，做的第一件事是 Within a year he turned the rundown house into a 17-room inn.（第 13 行），呼應 (A) Remodeled the house。
(B) Placed an ad in a magazine 是改建後才做的事。此外，Hobbs 並沒有做 (C) Asked for donations from his friends、(D) Paved a road to the inn 這兩件事。

---

4. 關於綠地旅館，文中可推論出什麼？

(A) 與卡尼斯村已有連接道路。　　　(B) 距離倫敦不遠。

(C) 受到鄉下人歡迎。　　　　　　　(D) 已經營業超過 30 年。

正確答案：B　　　　　　　　　　　　　　　　　　　　推論題

Grassy Meadows 是旅館（inn）名稱。這題要針對這間旅館，選出與本文內容相符的敘述。從第 16 行的 the inn soon became a popular spot for Londoners wanting a break from the city's fast pace without having to travel too far.，可知旅館位於倫敦不遠處，答案是 (B)。

ⓘwithout having to travel too far 表示距離不會太遠，呼應了 not far 這個選項。

單字

- article *(n.)* 文章，報導
- in the middle of nowhere 位於荒郊野外
- mere *(adj.)* 一點點的
- worth *(adj.)* 價值〜的
- population *(n.)* 人口
- assure *(v.)* 向（某人）保證（某事）
- recall *(v.)* 回想
- rundown *(adj.)* 荒廢的
- enthusiast *(n.)* 愛好者
  (adj.) enthusiastic 熱衷的
  (n.) enthusiasm 熱忱

- pave *(v.)* 舖設
- fully booked 預約已滿的
- in advance 預先
- prove *(v.)* 證明
- remodel *(v.)* 改建，改裝
- place an ad 刊登廣告
- donation *(n.)* 捐款，捐贈
  (v.) donate 捐款，捐贈
- rural area 郊區
- operate *(v.)* 營業

If you liked the film *Run South*, don't miss *Clouds of the Storm*, an earlier novel by Stan Bisbee now being shown on the big screen.

"Fans of *Run South* feel they're on familiar ground," according to award-winning director Mick Steward, who brought both Bisbee books to film. "The story concerns a secret society, a cleverly creative villain, and nonstop adventure mixed with a mystery that must be solved in a race against time."

Clouds of the Storm brings back adventurer Murdock Leonard as a younger man, played again by Han Waitsfield, who also narrates the film. As the film begins, Leonard finds himself trapped in a wooden box in a field in Uganda. Only remembering waking up sometime earlier in his New York City apartment for breakfast, Leonard must quickly find out why he was brought there and who is chasing him.

Leonard meets Wendy Fine, world traveler and treasure hunter, played by actress Lucy McGuire, who reveals Leonard's purpose for being in Africa during the roller-coaster plot that unfolds.

Through seven countries on three continents and with enough shady characters and fast-paced storytelling to keep you on the edge of your seat, this film will not disappoint. And Bisbee fans will also be very satisfied with how well Steward brings to life pages from the novel and how accurately the actors play their characters. *Clouds of the Storm* is sure to be this year's top summer hit and should not be missed.

5. Who is the narrator in the film?

(A) Lucy McGuire

(B) Mick Steward

(C) Han Waitsfield

(D) Stan Bisbee

6. What is indicated about the film?

(A) It is mainly about the beauty of African nature.

(B) It will be released at theaters in the winter.

(C) It is based on an award-winning novel.

(D) It is a work by the director of *Run South*.

做完之後，在下方表格填入作答時間與答對題數。

第**1**回 ＿＿＿月＿＿＿日	第**2**回 ＿＿＿月＿＿＿日	第**3**回 ＿＿＿月＿＿＿日
答對題數 ＿＿＿題 時間 ＿＿＿分＿＿＿秒	答對題數 ＿＿＿題 時間 ＿＿＿分＿＿＿秒	答對題數 ＿＿＿題 時間 ＿＿＿分＿＿＿秒

翻譯及解析

5-6 題參考以下評論。

> 如果你喜歡電影《奔向南方》，那你絕不能錯過現正上映、改編自 Stan Bisbee 前一部小說的《風暴雲》。
>
> 將 Bisbee 兩部小說搬上螢幕的得獎導演 Mike Steward 表示：「喜歡《奔向南方》的觀眾會覺得，這兩部電影很熟悉。故事是關於一個祕密組織與一名既聰明又有創造力的反派角色，在與時間賽跑的同時，還必須不斷冒險解開謎題。」
>
> 《風暴雲》回到冒險家 Murdock Leonard 年輕的過往，這個角色再次由 Han Waitsfield 飾演，他同時也是本片旁白。電影一開始，Leonard 發現自己被困在烏干達原野上的一個木箱裡。他只記得自己剛在紐約公寓醒來準備吃早餐。他得立即找出困在這裡的理由以及追殺他的幕後人物。
>
> Leonard 遇見了由 Lucy McGuire 所飾演的 Wendy Fine。她是周遊世界的尋寶人，隨著雲霄飛車般的劇情展開，她也將揭開 Leonard 之所以身處非洲的理由。
>
> 本片拍攝場景橫越三大洲七個國家，懸疑角色加上緊湊敘事節奏，會讓你興奮地坐不住，保證不會令你失望。Steward 完美賦予小說血肉，演員精準詮釋角色，相信會讓 Bisbee 的粉絲滿意。《風暴雲》無疑會是今夏最賣座的電影，千萬不要錯過。

5. 誰是電影旁白？

(A) Lucy McGuire

(B) Mick Steward

(C) Han Waitsfield

(D) Stan Bisbee

正確答案：C　　　　　　　　　　　　　　　　　　詢問細節

題目的 narrator「旁白」是解題關鍵字。從第三段第 3 行 Han Waitsfield, who also narrates the film.，可知 Han Waitsfield 是旁白，答案是 (C)。

① 題目的 narrator 是名詞，呼應文中的 narrate「擔任旁白」這個動詞。

6. 關於電影，文中提及什麼？

(A) 有關非洲美景。

(B) 會在冬天上映。

(C) 根據得獎小說改編。

(D)《奔向南方》的導演之作。

推論題

第一段提到 If you liked the film *Run South*, don't miss *Clouds of the Storm*, an earlier novel by Stan Bisbee now being shown on the big screen.，可知 *Run South* 和 *Clouds of the Storm* 兩部電影是翻拍自同一個作家（Stan Bisbee）的小說。此外，第二段第 1 行提到 "Fans of *Run South* feel they're on familiar ground," according to award-winning director Mick Steward, who brought both Bisbee books to film.，可看出兩部作品是由同一個導演（Mick Steward）拍攝，答案是 (D)。

ⓘ 文中採間接敘述，說明兩部作品的導演是同一人，需要花點工夫找出答案。

單字

- film *(n.)* 電影，影片
- novel *(n.)* 小說
- on the big screen（電影）上映中的
- award-winning *(adj.)* 獲獎的
- director *(n.)* 導演
  (v.) direct 導演
- concern *(v.)* 有關係
- secret society 祕密組織
- villain *(n.)* 反派角色
- adventure *(n.)* 冒險
  (n.) adventurer 冒險家
- race against time 與時間賽跑
- narrate *(v.)* 擔任旁白
  (n.) narrator 旁白

- trap *(v.)/(n.)* 設陷阱捕捉
  （常用作被動式）；陷阱
- chase *(v.)* 追逐
- reveal *(v.)* 揭開
- unfold *(v.)*（故事）展開
- continent *(n.)* 洲
- shady *(adj.)* 可疑的
- fast-paced *(adj.)* 步調快的
- bring ~ to life
  賦予～生命，使～變得生動
- on the edge of one's seat
  （因興奮激動）坐立不安

Richard Jones   1:37 P.M.
Janet, could you do me a favor?
After I got off the train at
Northborough Station, I realized I'd
left my briefcase on board.

Janet Taylor   1:40 P.M.
Sorry to hear that. What do you
need me to do?

Richard Jones   1:42 P.M.
I have an appointment with a
realtor to look at a piece of property
here in about twenty minutes.
I wrote down the address in my
notebook, but it's in my briefcase.
There's a schedule on the wall beside
my desk. It's written there too.

Janet Taylor   1:43 P.M.
Okay, I'm looking at it now. Should
I text it to you?

Richard Jones   1:45 P.M.
That would be great. The station
manager said my briefcase was
turned in a few stops from here,
but I'll have to wait until after my
appointment to pick it up.

7. What problem does Mr. Jones mention?

(A) He cannot find a train station.

(B) He has the wrong address.

(C) He lost possession of his briefcase.

(D) He is late for an appointment.

8. At 1:43 P.M., what does Ms. Taylor mean when she writes, "Okay, I'm looking at it now"?

(A) She is viewing a property.

(B) She has found an address.

(C) She can see a notebook.

(D) She has located a briefcase.

做完之後，在下方表格填入作答時間與答對題數。

第 **1** 回 _____月_____日	第 **2** 回 _____月_____日	第 **3** 回 _____月_____日
答對題數 _____題 時間 _____分_____秒	答對題數 _____題 時間 _____分_____秒	答對題數 _____題 時間 _____分_____秒

翻譯及解析

7-8 題參考以下文字簡訊串。

Richard Jones   下午 1 點 37 分

Janet，可以幫我個忙嗎？我在諾斯勃勒車站下車之後，才發現我把公事包忘在火車上了。

Janet Taylor   下午 1 點 40 分

很遺憾聽到這事。你需要我怎麼做？

Richard Jones   下午 1 點 42 分

20 分鐘後我要跟房仲去看一個物件。我在筆電上有寫下地址，不過筆電也放在公事包裡。我桌子旁的牆上有貼一張日程表，上面也有地址。

Janet Taylor   下午 1 點 43 分

好的，我現在看到了。用簡訊傳給你嗎？

Richard Jones   下午 1 點 45 分

好。車站人員說我的公事包已經找到，放在離這裡幾站的車站。但是我得等到碰面結束後才能去拿。

---

7. Jones 先生提到什麼問題？

(A) 他找不到火車站。

(B) 他搞錯地址。

(C) 他遺失公事包。

(D) 他會面遲到。

正確答案：C   詢問細節

Mr. Jones 在下午 1 點 37 分的時候傳訊息說 After I got off the train at Northborough Station, I realized I'd left my briefcase on board.，由此可知，他把公事包遺忘在車上，答案是 (C)。

① 這種聊天訊息的文章是新制題型，在 Part 7 固定出現兩篇。一篇簡單，一篇較難。

8. 下午 1 點 43 分的簡訊，Taylor 小姐寫「好的，我現在看到它了。」是什麼意思？

(A) 她正在參觀物件。

(B) 她找到住址了。

(C) 她可以看到筆電。

(D) 她找到公事包了。

正確答案：B

理解意圖

Mr. Jones 在下午 1 點 42 分傳訊息說 I wrote down the address in my notebook, but it's in my briefcase. There's a schedule on the wall beside my desk. It's written there too.，對此，Ms. Taylor 回覆 Okay, I'm looking at it now.。這裡的 it 指的是計畫表上所寫的地址，答案是 (B)。

ⓘ 本題是「理解意圖」題，也是新制多益 Part 7 新題型，如果題目出現類似這題的 it 代名詞，務必要確認 it 指的是哪個人事物。

單字

- get off 下（大眾交通工具）
- realize (v.) 發現
- on board 在車上
- appointment (n.) 會面
- realtor (n.) 房屋仲介
- text (v.)/(n.) 傳訊；文字訊息
- turn in 遞送

GETTING YOUR SOLAR LAMP GLOWING

You have purchased a Solar Lamp for your garden or yard. And with all-night lighting, uncomplicated installation, and no annoying wires,  you made the right landscaping choice! Now all you need to do to get your lamp glowing is follow the simple instructions below.

What to do:
Each lamp comes with a photo sensor, ground stake, two solar panels, and two rechargeable batteries. To assemble, insert the batteries at the back of the lamp. Next, slide the solar panels into the slots marked SP at the sides of the lamp. Attach the photo sensor to the lamp top by turning it clockwise over the red circle.

What next?
Your Solar Lamp should be placed out of the shade and where it can collect enough of the sun's rays. The sensor will automatically detect dusk or dawn and will turn on or off accordingly. The lamp can be affixed to a tree or post, or mounted on the stake, which should be pressed into soft earth.

9. For whom are the instructions probably intended?

(A) A purchaser

(B) A manufacturer

(C) A technician

(D) A retailer

10. What are readers instructed to do first with the lamp?

(A) Place it out of the shade

(B) Insert batteries at the back of the lamp

(C) Slide solar panels into slots

(D) Attach the photo sensor to the top

11. The word "assemble" in paragraph 2, line 3, is closest in meaning to

(A) set up

(B) pick up

(C) take place

(D) come along

做完之後，在下方表格填入作答時間與答對題數。

第 1 回 ＿＿月＿＿日	第 2 回 ＿＿月＿＿日	第 3 回 ＿＿月＿＿日
答對題數 ＿＿題 時間 ＿＿分＿＿秒	答對題數 ＿＿題 時間 ＿＿分＿＿秒	答對題數 ＿＿題 時間 ＿＿分＿＿秒

翻譯及解析

9-11 題參考以下說明書。

打開太陽能燈

您為自家庭院添購了太陽能燈。整晚照明、安裝簡易、沒有惱人的電線,本產品正是您造景的正確選擇!現在只需依照以下簡單指示,就能開始使用:

您需要:

每盞燈具都有 1 個影像感應器、1 根接地燈柱、2 塊太陽能板,以及 2 顆充電電池。安裝時先將電池放入燈具背面。接著將太陽能板插入燈具兩側標有 SP 的插槽,並將影像感應器以順時針方向轉入燈具頂部的紅色圓圈上方。

接下來:

太陽能燈應放置在能充分蒐集陽光的地方,避免放在陰暗處。感應器會自動偵測時間是黃昏或清晨,自動開關燈。燈具可固定在樹上或柱子上,或是安裝在接地燈柱上,再將燈柱插入鬆軟的泥土裡。

---

9. 這份指示可能是寫給誰看的?

(A) 購買人　　　　　　　　(B) 製造商

(C) 技師　　　　　　　　　(D) 零售商

正確答案:A　　　　　　　　　　　　　　　　　　詢問細節

題目關鍵字是 Who。開頭句 You have purchased a Solar Lamp for your garden or yard.,可知這份說明書是專門寫給購買 Solar Lamp 的人。此外,內容也是為消費者所寫,裡頭記載有關商品的基本事項,答案是 (A)。

①purchaser「購買人」指的是 purchase「購買」商品的人。

---

10. 讀者被指示要先對燈具做什麼?

(A) 放在陰暗處以外的地方　　　　(B) 將電池放入燈具背後

(C) 把太陽能板插入插槽　　　　　(D) 將影像感應器安裝在頂部

正確答案:B　　　　　　　　　　　　　　　　　　詢問細節

題目關鍵字是 what to do first「首先要做的事情」。小標「What to do:」下方文字說明第 1 個步驟是 To assemble, insert the batteries at the back of the lamp.,因此答案是 (B) Insert batteries at the back of the lamp。

11. 第二段第 3 行的 assemble 一字，意思最接近

(A) set up「組裝」

(B) pick up「撿起來」

(C) take place「舉行」

(D) come along「出現」

正確答案：A 同義字題

第二段第 3 行的 assemble 出現在 To assemble, insert the batteries at the back of the lamp. 這個句子裡，為「組裝」之意，與 (A) set up 的意思最接近。

單字

- instructions *(n.)*（常用複數型）
  說明書；說明，指示
  (v.) instruct 指示，指導
- solar *(adj.)* 太陽能的
- glow *(v.)* 發光
- purchase *(v.)* 購買
  (n.) purchaser 購買人
- installation *(n.)* 安裝
  (v.) install 安裝
- annoying *(adj.)* 惱人的
- landscaping *(n.)* 造景，景觀美化
- sensor *(n.)* 感應器
- ground stake 接地樁
- rechargeable *(adj.)* 可充電的
- assemble *(v.)* 組裝
  (n.) assembly 組裝

- insert *(v.)* 插入
- slide *(v.)* 使滑動
- slot *(n.)* 溝槽
- mark *(v.)* 做記號
- clockwise *(adv.)/(adj.)* 順時針
- automatically *(adv.)* 自動地
- detect *(v.)* 偵測
- dusk *(n.)* 黃昏
- dawn *(n.)* 黎明
- accordingly *(adv.)* 相應地；因此
- affix *(v.)* 使固定
- manufacturer *(n.)* 製造商
- set up 組裝
- come along（人）現身，
  （物）出現；跟隨

To: All Employees
Date: August 19

Our EMCI Digital Microscope has been on the market for 21 months now. —[1]—. Over this period, we have accumulated valuable feedback from people using it in various fields, from medical science to botany. Some of them have also pointed out problems with the microscope user manual. —[2]—. We will make changes to the instructions so that they are clearer and include more detailed descriptions where necessary. —[3]—.

If you have any suggestions for the manual, please call me in the R&D Department at extension 395. —[4]—. I will be overseeing the revisions and would appreciate your ideas for improvements before September 22.

Thank you.

Rebecca Barrett
Managing Director
APEX Solutions

12. What is the purpose of the memo?

    (A) To explain a customer satisfaction survey

    (B) To share details about a product test

    (C) To request the involvement of staff members

    (D) To recommend changes to a procedure

13. What is indicated about APEX Solutions?

    (A) Its customers work in different fields.

    (B) Its services will soon be expanding.

    (C) It will merge with another company.

    (D) It manufactures cleaning equipment.

14. In which of the positions marked [1], [2], [3], and [4] does the following sentence best belong?

    "Therefore, we have decided to update the content."

    (A) [1]

    (B) [2]

    (C) [3]

    (D) [4]

做完之後，在下方表格填入作答時間與答對題數。

第 1 回 ____月____日	第 2 回 ____月____日	第 3 回 ____月____日
答對題數 _____題 時間 _____分_____秒	答對題數 _____題 時間 _____分_____秒	答對題數 _____題 時間 _____分_____秒

翻譯及解析

12-14 題參考以下備忘錄。

收件人：全體員工

日期：8 月 19 日

我們的 EMCI 數位顯微鏡上市至今已經 21 個月。—[1]—這段期間，我們累積了來自各行各業使用者的寶貴意見，從醫療科學到植物學都有。部分使用者指出，使用說明書上有些問題。—[2]—我們將會修正使用說明書，讓它更清楚，並加入更多必要的詳細敘述。—[3]—

如果你對使用說明書有任何建議，請撥打研究開發部門分機 395。—[4]—我將負責監督所有修改內容，若能在 9 月 22 日前提供改善建議，我將不勝感激。

謝謝。

Rebecca Barrett

APEX Solutions 董事總經理

---

12. 此備忘錄的目的是？

(A) 說明客戶滿意度調查結果

(B) 分享產品報告細節

(C) 請求成員參與

(D) 建議變更一項步驟

正確答案：C　　　　　　　　　　　　　　　　　　　　　　　文章目的

寄件人在第一段提到，顯微鏡的 user manual「使用說明書」有問題，所以在第二段的第 1 行提出 If you have any suggestions for the manual, please call me in the R&D Department at extension 395.，希望徵求員工建議，答案是 (C)。選項 (C) To request the involvement of staff members「請求員工參與」，這裡使用了比較隱晦的說法來表達請求。

① 將正確選項改寫成較為隱晦的說法，模糊文中的具體資訊，是基本陷阱題。

13. 關於 APEX Solutions，文中提及什麼？

(A) 客戶來自各行各業。　　　　　　(B) 即將擴大服務範圍。

(C) 會與其他公司合併。　　　　　　(D) 製造清潔器材。

正確答案：A　　　　　　　　　　　　　　　　　　`選項對照`

找出符合本文的選項。從第一段第 2 行的 Over this period, we have accumulated valuable feedback from people using it in various fields, from medical science to botany. 可知顧客來自各行各業，答案是 (A)。文中的 people using it in various fields 在選項中被換句話說，改成 Its customers work in different fields。

---

14. 在標示 [1]、[2]、[3]、[4] 的位置中，何者適合放入以下句子？

「因此，我們決定更新內容。」

(A) [1]　　　　　　　　　　　　　　(B) [2]

(C) [3]　　　　　　　　　　　　　　(D) [4]

正確答案：B　　　　　　　　　　　　　　　　　　`插入句題`

插入句以 Therefore「因此」開頭，因此銜接在前的句子必須點出 we have decided to update the content 的原因。[2] 的前一句是 Some of them have also pointed out problems with the microscope user manual.，把插入句放進去後，整句話的意思就變成「由於用戶手冊有問題，因此我們決定更新內容」，可完美串起因果關係。

ⓘ 詢問某句子該安插入文章何處的題目，稱為「插入句題」，是多益新制 Part 6-7 的新題型，在 Part 7 會出現 2 題。本句的插入句句首是連接詞 Therefore「因此」，用來表示與前一句話的因果關係，為解題關鍵。

單字

- microscope *(n.)* 顯微鏡
- accumulate *(v.)* 收集，累積
- botany *(n.)* 植物學
- user manual 使用手冊
- R&D department　研究開發部
  （R&D = research and development）
- extension *(n.)* 分機
- oversee *(v.)* 監督
- revision *(n.)* 修訂
- managing director 董事總經理
- involvement *(n.)* 參與
- merge *(v.)* 合併

GRAND PEGASUS HOTEL

The 22-story Grand Pegasus Hotel offers all the amenities that make a business trip more comfortable, convenient, and productive. Located in the heart of Miami and just 12 miles from the airport, this hotel is ideal for every business traveler. Our airport shuttle is available at no charge, taking guests to and from the hotel twice an hour. Guest services also include use of our business center, swimming pool, and fitness club, all open around the clock. And our business center is always ready to handle your copying, printing, and shipping needs.

The Grand Pegasus has 82,000 square feet of meeting and event space, including a ballroom for 2,500 guests. We can also provide catering, staffing, and audiovisual equipment services for your event.

Enhancing Your Business Trip

Room Amenities

Free Internet access, LCD TV with movie channels (fees apply), cordless and speaker phone, complimentary newspaper, radio with alarm clock, coffeemaker, and more

- Smoking is allowed only in designated outdoor areas.

- Children ten years old or younger are not permitted in the pool without adult supervision.

- Check-in time begins at 3:00 P.M.

- Check-out is by noon.

15. For whom is the advertisement most likely intended?

    (A) School groups

    (B) Hotel managers

    (C) Business travelers

    (D) Foreign tourists

16. According to the advertisement, what does the hotel NOT offer for free?

    (A) Airport shuttle transportation

    (B) Internet access

    (C) A newspaper

    (D) Movie channels

17. What is indicated about the hotel?

    (A) Smoking is permitted in its business center.

    (B) Its fitness club closes at midnight.

    (C) Its airport shuttle departs twice daily.

    (D) Ten-year-olds can use its pool with a parent.

做完之後，在下方表格填入作答時間與答對題數。

第 1 回 ＿＿＿月＿＿＿日	第 2 回 ＿＿＿月＿＿＿日	第 3 回 ＿＿＿月＿＿＿日
答對題數 ＿＿＿題 時間 ＿＿＿分＿＿＿秒	答對題數 ＿＿＿題 時間 ＿＿＿分＿＿＿秒	答對題數 ＿＿＿題 時間 ＿＿＿分＿＿＿秒

翻譯及解析

15-17 題參考以下廣告。

Pegasus 大飯店
升級您的出差旅程

位於邁阿密市中心、22 層樓高的 Pegasus 大飯店，提供能讓您的商務出差更為舒適、便利且有效率的所有設施。本飯店距離機場僅 12 英里，是商務人士的理想住處。我們提供每小時兩班、免費往返於機場與飯店的接駁巴士。賓客能使用我們 24 小時全天開放的商務中心、游泳池與健身俱樂部。商務中心也能處理您的影印、印刷與寄件需求。

Pegasus 大飯店擁有八萬二千平方英尺的開會與活動空間，其中包含可容納 2,500 位賓客的宴會廳，並提供外燴、人力服務與音響視聽設備，能滿足您的活動需求。

客房設施：
免費網路，可觀看電影頻道（需付費）的液晶電視，無線免持電話，免費報紙，有鬧鐘功能的收音機，咖啡機，以及更多。

- 只有指定戶外區允許吸菸。
- 10 歲以下孩童，無成人監督不得進入泳池。
- 入住時間下午 3 點
- 退房時間中午 12 點

---

15. 這則廣告最有可能給誰看？

(A) 學校團體
(B) 飯店經理
(C) 出差人士
(D) 外國旅客

正確答案：C　　　　　　　　　　　　　　　　**文章主旨**

從第一段的 make a business trip more comfortable, convenient, and productive 與 ideal for every business traveler 等句子，可知這篇廣告的目標族群是商務人士，答案是 (C)。

ⓘ 「這篇文章是寫給誰看？」這類問題，需掌握文章大意來解題。此外，文中所使用的關鍵字也是線索，如這題的 business trip、business traveler 等。

16. 根據廣告，以下何者非飯店免費提供？

(A) 機場交通接駁

(B) 網路

(C) 報紙

(D) 電影頻道

正確答案：D

本題詢問「非」免費的東西。從 Room Amenities「客房設施」下方的 movie channels (fees apply)，可看出電影頻道需要付費，答案是 (D)。

ⓘfees apply 指的是「適用費用」，意即「需付費」。

---

17. 關於飯店，文中提到什麼？

(A) 商務中心允許吸菸。

(B) 健身房夜晚關閉。

(C) 機場接駁巴士一天兩個班次。

(D) 10 歲孩童有家長陪同可使用泳池。

正確答案：D

選擇與內文相符的選項。Room Amenities 第 2 點說明提到 Children ten years old or younger are not permitted in the pool without adult supervision.「10 歲以下的孩童不得在無大人監督的情況下使用游泳池」。表示只要有大人陪同就能使用游泳池，答案是 (D)。

ⓘChildren ten years old or younger 是指「含 10 歲以下的孩童」。

單字

- enhance *(v.)* 提升，加強
- 22-story *(adj.)* 22 層樓高的
- amenity *(n.)* 便利設施
- productive *(adj.)* 多產的
- airport shuttle 機場接駁巴士
- around the clock 全天運作的
- shipping *(n.)* 運送
- square feet 平方英尺
- ballroom *(n.)* 宴會廳
- catering *(n.)* 外燴服務
- staffing *(n.)* 人員配備
- audiovisual equipment 音響視聽設備
- LCD TV 液晶電視，
  LCD 為 liquid crystal display 縮寫
- fees apply 需付費
- speaker phone 免持電話
- complimentary *(adj.)* 免費的
- allow *(v.)* 允許
- designated *(adj.)* 指定的
- outdoor *(adj.)* 戶外的
- permit *(v.)* 允許
- supervision *(n.)* 監督
  (v.) supervise 監督
- depart *(v.)* 出發

Monday, October 31

Dear Mr. Watson:

Thank you for spending some of your valuable time attending my lecture in Melbourne last month. It was a pleasure to speak with you after the lecture about your new business. I am very sorry for this late reply. After leaving Australia, I went to Tokyo, Seoul, and Beijing to do a series of business presentations and did not have a spare moment to reply to you.

I am very interested in your offer and would like to discuss the possibility of going over it further with you. I am now in Singapore and will be here until the end of the week, at which time I will be flying to Bali for a ten-day vacation with my family. I will be back in Melbourne, however, on December 6 and would like to meet with you before the end of the year. I would also appreciate seeing a draft of your business plan, including a proposed schedule and an estimate on startup costs. You can bring it to our meeting.

Please let me know the date, place, and time of the meeting by e-mail.

I look forward to hearing from you soon.

Sincerely,

Robert Barnegat

Robert Barnegat

18. What did Robert Barnegat do in Seoul?

(A) He attended an international convention.

(B) He gave a business presentation.

(C) He took a vacation with his family.

(D) He drafted proposals for Mr. Watson.

19. Where did Robert Barnegat meet Mr. Watson?

(A) Singapore

(B) Beijing

(C) Melbourne

(D) Tokyo

20. Why has Robert Barnegat been unable to reply to Mr. Watson?

(A) He has been on vacation with his family.

(B) He has been on a business trip in Asia.

(C) He has been waiting for a production estimate.

(D) He has been busy preparing for some lectures.

21. When does Robert Barnegat want to discuss business with Mr. Watson?

(A) In October

(B) In November

(C) In December

(D) In January

做完之後，在下方表格填入作答時間與答對題數。

第 1 回 ＿＿＿月＿＿＿日	第 2 回 ＿＿＿月＿＿＿日	第 3 回 ＿＿＿月＿＿＿日
答對題數 ＿＿＿題 時間 ＿＿＿分＿＿＿秒	答對題數 ＿＿＿題 時間 ＿＿＿分＿＿＿秒	答對題數 ＿＿＿題 時間 ＿＿＿分＿＿＿秒

翻譯及解析

18-21 題參考以下信件。

---

10 月 31 日星期一

親愛的 Watson 先生：

感謝您上個月抽出寶貴時間，參加我在墨爾本的演講。我很高興能在演講結束後，跟您談談您的新事業。

很抱歉這封信回覆有點晚。離開澳洲之後，我前往東京、首爾以及北京進行一系列的商務簡報，因此無法抽空回覆。

我對您的提案相當感興趣，想進一步談談可能性。我現在人在新加坡，會待到這個週末，接著會飛到峇厘島開始 10 天的家族旅行。不過，我會在 12 月 6 日返回墨爾本，希望可以在今年底前與您碰面。若能看看您的公司計畫草案，包含創業進度表與創業成本估價，我將會不勝感激。您可以在見面時帶過來。

請透過電子郵件讓我知道會面的日期、地點與時間。

期待很快收到您的消息。

Robert Barnegat 謹啟

---

18. Robert Barnegat 在首爾做了什麼？

(A) 參加國際研討會。

(B) 做商務簡報。

(C) 跟家人度假。

(D) 為 Watson 先生草擬提案。

正確答案：B　　　　　　　　　　　　　　　　　　　詢問細節

題目詢問寄信人 Robert Barnegat 在 Seoul 做了什麼事。用 Seoul 這個關鍵字回去看內文的話，可發現第一段的 6 行提到 I went to Tokyo, Seoul, and Beijing to do a series of business presentations。可知他在首爾做了商業簡報，答案是 (B)。

19. Robert Barnegat 是在哪裡跟 Watson 先生碰面的？

(A) 新加坡   (B) 北京

(C) 墨爾本   (D) 東京

正確答案：C   詢問細節

從第一段 1 行的 Thank you for spending some of your valuable time attending my lecture in Melbourne last month. It was a pleasure to speak with you after the lecture about your new business. 可知他們已經在 (C) Melbourne 見過面。

---

20. Robert Barnegat 為什麼無法回覆 Watson 先生？

(A) 他跟家人正在度假。

(B) 他在亞洲出差。

(C) 他在等產品估價單。

(D) 他忙著準備演說。

正確答案：B   詢問細節

Robert Barnegat 在第一段後半段為晚回信道歉後，說明了晚回信的原因。他說 After leaving Australia, I went to Tokyo, Seoul, and Beijing to do a series of business presentations and did not have a spare moment to reply to you.，答案是 (B)。

---

21. Robert Barnegat 何時想跟 Watson 先生討論事業？

(A) 10 月   (B) 11 月

(C) 12 月   (D) 1 月

正確答案：C   詢問細節

從第二段 6 行的 I will be back in Melbourne, however, on December 6 and would like to meet with you before the end of the year. 可知 Robert Barnegat 在 December 6 回來，希望年底前見面，答案是 (C)。

①此題組的每個問題都與人名有關，可見在作答前弄清楚寄件人與收件人是基本功。

單字

- spare moment 空閒
- offer *(n.)* 提議
- startup cost 創業成本
- convention *(n.)* 大型會議、集會
- on a business trip 因商外出，出差

ERIC DAVIS [11:01 A.M.]
Hi all. I'd like to know how preparations for next month's trade show are going. Are we still on schedule?

JIM COCHRANE [11:02 A.M.]
We planned out the booth, and it's going to look awesome. All our new exercise machines will be on display.

DONNA WRIGHT [11:03 A.M.]
We haven't decided on a game yet, though. I want something big and colorful so that it catches everyone's attention. But some people on the marketing team don't see the point of having one.

ANNETT LEWIS [11:04 A.M.]
Well, I get it. But we'll be letting visitors try out the bikes and other machines. That alone will draw plenty of interest to the booth.

DONNA WRIGHT [11:05 A.M.]
But we should use a game to give out coupons for our products. Plus, games make it easier to start up conversations with potential customers.

JIM COCHRANE [11:06 A.M.]
And we want people to submit their business cards for a chance to win a big gift at the end of the show. How about a prize wheel? They're eye-catching and amusing.

22. What is the group planning to do?

(A) Conduct some market research

(B) Photocopy some schedules

(C) Promote some products

(D) Pass out business cards

23. At 11:04 A.M., what does Ms. Lewis most likely mean when she writes, "I get it"?

(A) She is in charge of picking up some items.

(B) She understands that games are useful.

(C) She knows how to use some equipment.

(D) She has figured out the meaning of a joke.

24. What is mentioned about the exercise machines?

(A) They can be used at a trade show.

(B) They are being sold at a discount price.

(C) They will be replaced immediately.

(D) They were delivered to a venue.

25. According to Ms. Wright, how can games be used?

(A) To attract new members

(B) To motivate employees

(C) To encourage exercise

(D) To initiate conversations

做完之後，在下方表格填入作答時間與答對題數。

第 1 回 _____月_____日	第 2 回 _____月_____日	第 3 回 _____月_____日
答對題數 _____題 時間 _____分_____秒	答對題數 _____題 時間 _____分_____秒	答對題數 _____題 時間 _____分_____秒

翻譯及解析

22-25 題參考以下線上聊天室。

ERIC DAVIS [11:01 A.M.]

哈囉大家，我想知道下個月貿易展的提案進度。我們有按照進度進行嗎？

JIM COCHRANE [11:02 A.M.]

我們想到設置展示間，看起來會很不錯。也能展示我們新推出的運動器材。

DONNA WRIGHT [11:03 A.M.]

但我們還沒選定遊戲。我想要又大又鮮豔的，才能吸引目光。不過行銷單位的部分同仁認為沒必要。

ANNETT LEWIS [11:04 A.M.]

但我明白。我們可以讓訪客試用腳踏車與其他器材。這樣的話，也能吸引大批人氣到來我們展區。

DONNA WRIGHT [11:05 A.M.]

不過我們應該設計遊戲，才能送出產品折價券。而且，遊戲也方便我們跟潛力顧客開啟話題。

JIM COCHRANE [11:06 A.M.]

我們想讓訪客用提供名片的方式，換取在節目尾聲贏得大獎的機會。獎品轉盤如何？既吸睛又好玩。

---

22. 這個團隊打算做什麼？

(A) 執行市場調查

(B) 影印進度表

(C) 促銷商品

(D) 遞名片

正確答案：C 文章目的

從交談內容可得知，他們所任職的公司將在下個月參加展覽會。參展目的是為了促進商品銷售，因此答案是 (C)。All our new exercise machines will be on display. 和 we'll be letting visitors try out the bikes and other machines 等句子也是線索。

①新制 Part 7 題型也會出現 3 人以上的線上聊天。

23. 早上 11 點 04 分，Lewis 小姐寫了「我懂了」，最有可能是什麼意思？

(A) 她負責挑選某些品項。

(B) 她明白遊戲是有用的。

(C) 她知道如何使用器材。

(D) 她明白笑話意思。

正確答案：B　　　　　　　　　　　　　　　　**理解意圖**

Annett Lewis 看到 Donna Wright 在上午 11 點 3 分傳的訊息 But some people on the marketing team don't see the point of having one.，所以回了 I get it.，這裡可以解釋成「儘管有人不懂遊戲進行的意義，但我能理解」，答案是 (B)。

ⓘ 這種「理解意圖」題需找出在對話背後的真正意思，請勿只看對話內容就作答。因為光是 I get it. 一句話就有多種涵義，請選擇「與上下文相符的選項」。

. . . .

24. 關於運動器材，文中提到什麼？

(A) 貿易展上可以使用。

(B) 會以低價促銷。

(C) 會立即更換。

(D) 會寄送到會場。

正確答案：A　　　　　　　　　　　　　　　　**選項對照**

從 Jim Cochrane 在上午 11 點 2 分傳的 All our new exercise machines will be on display. 可知，展覽上將會展出所有新的健身器材。此外，Annett Lewis 在上午 11 點 4 分回覆：But we'll be letting visitors try out the bikes and other machines.，可知參觀民眾可試用機器，答案是 (A)。

ⓘ trade show「貿易展」現場不會販售產品，展出產品的目的是為了獲得既有客戶的訂單、增加新客戶。

25. 根據 Wright 小姐，遊戲是用來做什麼的？

(A) 吸引新會員

(B) 激勵士氣

(C) 鼓勵運動

(D) 開啟對話

詢問細節

正確答案：**D**

Donna Wright 在上午 11 點 5 分傳訊息說：games make it easier to start up conversations with potential customers. 「用來開啟對話」，因此答案是 (D)。

ⓘ 選項只是把 start up conversations 用 To initiate conversations 換句話說。

單字

- trade show 貿易展
- on schedule 進度如期的
- plan out 籌劃
- booth (n.)（展場）棚位；電話亭
- decide on 選定
- see the point of 理解～的重要性
- draw (v.) 吸引（注意）
- interest (n.) 關心
- conversation (n.) 會話
- photocopy (v.)/(n.) 影印

- promote (v.) 促銷
- pass out 發放
- in charge of 負責～
- figure out 理解
- discount (n.) 折扣
- deliver (v.) 寄送
- venue (n.) 會場
- motivate (v.) 激勵
- encourage (v.) 鼓勵
- initiate (v.) 開始

NOTE

Streetcars to Make Comeback in Bretford

Nearly 60 years after Bretford closed its streetcar network, the city is set to open a new line in its central business district. Beginning on May 12, red streetcars will run between Union Station on Wilson Avenue and Hillview Plaza on Greensboro Road. —[1]—. The line, which cost $48 million to build, is approximately 1.8 miles long.

Bus service along the same route will not be affected by the streetcars. —[2]—. Passengers with a transfer ticket will be able to switch between streetcars and some buses. Moreover, the new line will operate from 6:30 A.M. to midnight, running one hour later than city buses. —[3]—.

A ribbon-cutting ceremony will be held at Union Station at 2:00 P.M. on May 10, during which Mayor Paul Bailey along with the director of the city's transit authority will commemorate the completion of the new line. —[4]—. It will include speeches, music, and free streetcar rides.

26. What is the article about?

(A) The launch of a new product

(B) A new transportation system

(C) Bus fare changes in Bretford

(D) A partnership between companies

27. What is indicated about the buses?

(A) They will operate on a revised schedule.

(B) They used to be a different color.

(C) They are mainly used by tourists.

(D) They stop running before midnight.

28. According to the article, what will happen on May 10?

(A) A city official will attend an event.

(B) Tickets will go on sale.

(C) A construction project will start.

(D) Staff training sessions will end.

29. In which of the positions marked [1], [2], [3], and [4] does the following sentence best belong?

"The general public is welcome to join the celebration."

(A) [1]

(B) [2]

(C) [3]

(D) [4]

第 1 回 _____月_____日	第 2 回 _____月_____日	第 3 回 _____月_____日
答對題數 _____題 時間 _____分_____秒	答對題數 _____題 時間 _____分_____秒	答對題數 _____題 時間 _____分_____秒

翻譯及解析

26-29 題參考以下報導。

貝雷德福路面電車再次復出

在貝雷德福關閉路面電車系統將近 60 年後的今天，將開通通往商業區的一條新路線。自 5 月 12 日起，紅色車身的路面電車會往返於統一車站的 Wilson 大道與 Hillview 購物中心的 Greensboro 路。—[1]—這條花了四千八百萬打造的路線，長約 1.8 英里。

行駛於同一路線的公車將不會受到影響。—[2]—有乘車票的乘客可以在路面電車與多條公車路線之間轉乘。此外，新路線的營運時間為早上 6 點 30 分到凌晨 12 點，比市公車多一小時。—[3]—

剪綵儀式將在 5 月 10 日下午 2 點於統一車站舉行，期間市長 Paul Bailey 與交通局長將會慶祝此路線竣工。—[4]—活動將包含演說、音樂會與路面電車免費搭乘體驗。

---

26. 這個報導有關什麼？

(A) 推出新產品　　　　　　　　　(B) 新的運輸系統
(C) 貝雷德福的公車費用變更　　　(D) 公司締結夥伴關係

正確答案：B　　　　　　　　　　　　　　　　　文章主旨

這篇報導談論新的路面電車。路面電車屬於大眾運輸系統，因此可以說是 (B) A new transportation system「新的運輸系統」。

①streetcar「路面電車」一字曾經出現在 Part 1 圖片描述題。

---

27. 關於公車，本文提到什麼？

(A) 將會以修正後的時刻表營運。　(B) 以前車身是其他顏色。
(C) 主要給觀光客搭乘。　　　　　(D) 凌晨 12 點前停駛。

正確答案：D　　　　　　　　　　　　　　　　　選項對照

題目關鍵字是 bus，請在文中尋找跟 bus 有關的訊息。第二段 4 行提到 the new line will operate from 6:30 A.M. to midnight, running one hour later than city buses.，可知公車比凌晨 12 點停開的路面電車還早一小時停開，答案是 (D)。midnight 一詞指的是「午夜 12 點整」。

28. 根據報導，5 月 10 日會發生什麼事？

(A) 市府官員會參加活動。

(B) 開賣車票。

(C) 建築工程開工。

(D) 員工訓練結束。

正確答案：A

從第三段 1 行的 A ribbon-cutting ceremony will be held at Union Station at 2:00 P.M. on May 10, during which Mayor Paul Bailey along with the director of the city's transit authority will commemorate the completion of the new line. ，可知市長與交通局長會出席 5 月 10 日的剪綵儀式，答案是 (A)。

ⓘ official 當名詞時，指團體中擔任要職的人，因此 city official 就是「市府官員」，director of the city's transit authority 等於「市政府交通局長」。

29. 在標示 [1]、[2]、[3]、[4] 的位置中，何者適合放入以下句子？

「歡迎一般大眾參與。」

(A) [1]

(B) [2]

(C) [3]

(D) [4]

正確答案：D

插入句中有 the celebration「慶祝活動」這個字，所以這句話的前後句理應要有與慶祝活動相關的內容。第三段的 A ribbon-cutting ceremony will be held at Union Station at 2:00 P.M. on May 10, during which Mayor Paul Bailey along with the director of the city's transit authority will commemorate the completion of the new line. 是有關慶祝活動的敘述，把 [4] 放進去後，整段就成了文意通順的句子：「5 月 10 日舉行剪綵儀式，歡迎民眾前往共襄盛舉」。

ⓘ 插入句下一句的人稱代名詞 It，指的正是插入句的 the celebration，也是解題線索。

單字

- streetcar *(n.)* 路面電車
- be set to 即將 = be about to
- district *(n.)* 地區
- approximately *(adv.)* 大約
- route *(n.)* 路線
- affect *(v.)* 影響
- passenger *(n.)* 乘客
- transfer *(n.)* 轉乘
- moreover *(adv.)* 再者
- midnight *(n.)* 凌晨 12 點，午夜
- ribbon-cutting ceremony
  剪綵儀式，啟用儀式
- transit authority 交通局
- commemorate *(v.)* 慶祝，紀念
- completion *(n.)* 完成
- go on sale 發售
- construction *(n.)* 建築工程
- general public 一般民眾

NOTE

) Aakarsh Online Furniture Catalog

Having trouble finding the perfect espresso table, a desk with the shade of beige that's just right for your office, or an amber table to bring life to a dreary corner?

Your search is over! Aakarsh Furniture is your craft company for manufacturing Indian furniture, antique reproduction furniture, trunks, beds, armoires, cabinets, and tables the way you want. And Aakarsh's online catalog is the place where the design of your custom-made Indian furniture begins. With a few simple clicks, select from various shades, styles, woods, and sizes, and even choose to view an image of your

 designed piece before placing an order. A range of elegant brass and iron fittings are also available to look at and select from.

Online or in our stores, we make quality for your comfort and distinctive taste. Because we understand that good sense combined with a timeless style is always in fashion, Aakarsh Furniture is confidently ready to serve all your furniture needs. To get started, click on any of the categories on this Web page.

Thank you for taking the time to visit Aakarsh Furniture's online catalog. For more information, call our customer service at 555-238-4981. For large orders (more than 10 pieces) please contact Aadi Nayar at: furniture@aakarsh.in

We guarantee a response to your inquiry within 24 hours.

To: Aadi Nayar

From: Emma McCormick

Subject: An Order

Date: 8 August

Dear Mr. Nayar:

We are a consulting firm based in London and would like tables with matching chairs for our meeting rooms. We are interested in ordering your Classic Dakota Tables along with Taj Crown Chairs. But we would like some information before we consider placing an order.

First, are the chairs and tables a good match? We are worried that the chairs may be too big for the tables. Also, after experimenting with your online catalog and using the furniture design function, we did not see mahogany brown as a choice for the tables we want. Does this mean they are not made in this colour?

Finally, because our office is moving to a new location at the end of October, we would like the tables and chairs in our hands at the new location just before we move there. Is this possible?

I will be away on holiday for ten days starting the day after tomorrow and will not be receiving e-mail while I'm away. So, I would appreciate your sending us an estimate as soon as possible. My assistant Keith Phelps knows that I have contacted you, so please send him an e-mail either this week or next at:
phelps@barnabyconsulting.uk
He will be taking care of this matter during my absence.

Best Regards,

Emma McCormick
CEO
Barnaby Consulting, Ltd.

30. What is the purpose of the advertisement?

    (A) To promote a business
    (B) To recruit new employees
    (C) To seek sales agents
    (D) To publicize an exhibition

31. When will Emma McCormick most likely receive a response from Aakarsh Furniture?

    (A) Within one day
    (B) The day after tomorrow
    (C) While she is on vacation
    (D) After ten days

32. According to the e-mail, what is the company concerned about?

    (A) The size of the chairs
    (B) The length of the tables
    (C) The color of the chairs
    (D) The weight of the tables

33. What can Aakarsh Furniture customers NOT see on the Web site?
    (A) A selection of wood types
    (B) A range of brass fittings
    (C) A list of shipping prices
    (D) A furniture design function

34. What can be inferred about Emma McCormick?
    (A) She wants to receive her order as soon as possible.
    (B) She plans to purchase more than ten pieces of furniture.
    (C) She is an executive member of a furniture retailer.
    (D) She expects Aadi Nayar to contact her during her vacation.

做完之後，在下方表格填入作答時間與答對題數。

第 1 回 _____月_____日	第 2 回 _____月_____日	第 3 回 _____月_____日
答對題數 _____題 時間 _____分_____秒	答對題數 _____題 時間 _____分_____秒	答對題數 _____題 時間 _____分_____秒

翻譯及解析

30-34 題參考以下廣告與電子郵件。

Aakarsh 線上家具型錄

還在苦苦找尋完美的咖啡桌、適合辦公室的象牙白書桌、或是能替沈悶角落添加活力的琥珀色餐桌嗎？

你不必再苦苦尋找了。Aakarsh 家具是一家能依照需求打造印度風家具、仿古家具、木箱、床組、衣櫥、櫃子與桌子的工藝公司。就從 Aakarsh 的線上型錄，量身訂做印度風家具吧。只要用滑鼠點幾下，就能在各種顏色、風格、木材與尺寸中做挑選，甚至也能在下單前預覽先前設計的家具圖片。本站也有一系列優雅的黃銅與鐵件供你瀏覽選購。

不管是在線上或實體店面，我們都追求舒適與獨到品味，製作高品質的產品。因為我們明白，好品味加上歷久不衰的風格，是永不退流行的，而 Aakarsh 家具能有自信地說，我們已經準備好滿足你的家具需求。點擊網頁上的類別開始吧。

感謝你花時間瀏覽 Aakarsh 線上家具型錄。如需更多資訊，請撥打服務專線 555-238-4981。大宗採購（超過 10 件商品）請寫信到 furniture@aakarsh.in 給 Aadi Nayar。

我們保證在 24 小時內回覆訊息。

30. 廣告的目的為何？

(A) 促銷事業
(B) 招募新員工
(C) 尋找經銷商
(D) 宣傳展覽

正確答案：A　　　　　　　　　　　　　文章目的

從標題 Aakarsh Online Furniture Catalog 以及全文得知，這篇廣告是由家具販售店刊登，用來招攬客人。答案是 (A) To promote a business。

① 選項中的 promote 與 publicize 都是當「宣傳」的意思，是多益常見單字。

31. Emma McCormick 最可能在何時收到 Aakarsh 家具的回覆？

    (A) 一天之內

    (B) 後天

    (C) 在她放假期間

    (D) 10 天後

正確答案：A　　　　　　　　　　　　　　　　　　　　詢問細節

題目的 When 是解題關鍵字，廣告最後寫到 We guarantee a response to your inquiry within 24 hours.，可推測店家會在一天內回信。答案是 (A)。

---

32. 根據電子郵件，公司擔心什麼事？

    (A) 椅子大小

    (B) 桌子長度

    (C) 椅子顏色

    (D) 桌子重量

正確答案：A　　　　　　　　　　　　　　　　　　　　詢問細節

題目的 concerned「擔心」是解題關鍵字，呼應了電子郵件第二段 2 行的 We are worried that the chairs may be too big for the tables.，答案是 (A)。

①問題的 concerned 和內文的 worried 都是「擔心」的意思。

---

33. Aakarsh 家具的客戶不會在網站上看到什麼？

    (A) 木材種類一覽表

    (B) 一系列的黃銅配件

    (C) 運費表

    (D) 家具設計功能

正確答案：C　　　　　　　　　　　　　　　　　　　　NOT 題

(A) A selection of wood types 和 (B) A range of brass fittings 呼應廣告第二段第 7 行 的 With a few simple clicks, select from various shades, styles, woods... A range of elegant brass and iron fittings are also available；(D) A furniture design function 則呼應了電子郵件第二段 3 行的 your online catalog and using the furniture design function。只有 (C) A list of shipping prices 未被提及。

34. 關於 Emma McCormick，從文中可推論出什麼？

(A) 她想儘快收到訂單。

(B) 她想購買 10 件以上的家具。

(C) 她是家具零售店的主管。

(D) 她希望 Aadi Nayar 會在她放假期間聯絡她。

正確答案：B　　　　　　　　　　　　　　　　　　　　**整合資訊**

這是封 Emma McCormick 寫給 Aadi Nayar 的電子郵件。廣告第四段 4 行提到 For large orders (more than 10 pieces) please contact Aadi Nayar at: furniture@aakarsh. in，可得知 Emma McCormick 想訂購 10 件以上的家具。因此答案是 (B)。

① 這題有難度，題目問的是 Emma McCormick 的事，所以會看她寫的電子郵件尋找線索。但這題光看電子郵件是沒辦法作答的，必須看過兩篇文章，才能推敲出關聯：想購買 10 件以上家具的顧客可寄電子郵件給 Aadi Nayar → Emma McCormick 寄電子郵件給 Aadi Nayar → Emma McCormick 想購買 10 件以上家具。

單字

- have trouble + Ving 做～遇到困難
- shade (n.) 色調；陰影
- amber (adj.)/(n.) 琥珀色的；琥珀
- dreary (adj.) 沈悶的
- craft (n.) 手工藝
- antique (adj.)/(n.) 古董的；古董
- reproduction (n.) 複製品
- armoire (n.) 衣櫃
- custom-made (adj.) 訂製的
- cabinet (n.) 櫥櫃
- a range of 各種的
- elegant (adj.) 優雅的
- brass (n.) 黃銅
- fitting (n.) 配件，附件
- quality (n.) 品質
- distinctive (adj.) 有特色的

- combine (v.) 結合
- serve a need 滿足需求
- take the time + to V 花費時間做～
- guarantee (v.) 保證
- inquiry (n.) 詢問
  (v.) inquire 詢問
- consulting firm 顧問公司
- matching (adj.) 匹配的
- consider (v.) 考慮
- assistant (n.) 助理
- take care of 處理，負責
- absence (n.) 缺席
  (adj.) absent 缺席的
- sales agent 經銷商
- concerned (adj.) 擔心的
- shipping price 運費

Daffodil Museum Membership

Your support is appreciated

☞ What do members receive?

- Free admission to the museum for you and one accompanied guest (All memberships)

- 15% off all shop purchases (Family and Patron)

- *Times of the Winds* magazine (with the *Daffodil Newsletter*) sent each quarter (Individual, Family, and Patron)

- Invitations and free admission to special events at the museum (Patron)

☞ Where does membership money go?

All membership fees go into the general funds of the museum. As a not-for-profit organization, the museum gets most of its revenue through donations. However, funds need to be raised from admissions, shop sales, and museum membership to help cover running costs.

☞ How much does it cost annually?

There are four levels of membership, as follows.

$20	Student / Senior Citizen
$30	Individual
$50	Family
$250	Patron

If you become a Patron or make a large donation, and you are a taxpayer in the USA, you will be able to claim tax benefits (contact the museum for further information).

☞ How are membership fees paid?

Please send your fee via check or money order to:
Daffodil Museum Friends
c/o Dr. Martin J. Druthers
1206 Charleston St.
Austin, TX 72800
USA

January 17

Daffodil Museum Board of Trustees
c/o Dr. Martin J. Druthers
1206 Charleston St.
Austin, TX 72800, USA

Dear Dr. Druthers and the Daffodil Museum
Board of Trustees:

My wife and I came home on Wednesday,
January 12, opened a letter from the Daffodil
Museum, and were disappointed to discover that
we were being invited to the Daffodil Museum
Ball for a charge of $100 per plate.

We have both paid $250 annually for nearly
four years, have regularly donated money to
the museum, and have never been charged for
the annual ball. However, what surprised us
more was the absence of an explanation telling
members why they are being charged this year.
I am certain that my late grandfather, who

donated large sums to the museum after its founding, would be disappointed as well.

What's more, we have not received *Times of the Winds* for over half a year. And the last time I visited the museum, with two friends, we embarrassingly had to wait ten minutes at the admission counter while our membership numbers were being verified.

A museum must be a responsible member of the community. To promote activities and then not follow through with them is irresponsible. I expect a letter of apology including an explanation for why we are being charged for this year's ball.

Sincerely,

Taylor White

Taylor White

35. What is the purpose of the letter?
    (A) To request a discount
    (B) To cancel a membership
    (C) To reject a donation
    (D) To make a complaint

36. What type of membership does Taylor White have?
    (A) Student / Senior Citizen
    (B) Individual
    (C) Family
    (D) Patron

37. How many magazines did the museum neglect to send Taylor White?
    (A) One
    (B) Two
    (C) Three
    (D) Four

38. In the letter, the word "absence" in paragraph 2, line 5, is closest in meaning to
    (A) abstract
    (B) detail
    (C) lack
    (D) presence

39. In the letter, what is NOT indicated about Taylor White?
    (A) He was invited to the annual ball for free last year.
    (B) He received slow service during his last visit to the museum.
    (C) He has been a museum member for almost four years.
    (D) He has a grandfather who is also disappointed with the poor treatment.

做完之後，在下方表格填入作答時間與答對題數。

第 1 回 ＿＿＿月＿＿＿日	第 2 回 ＿＿＿月＿＿＿日	第 3 回 ＿＿＿月＿＿＿日
答對題數 ＿＿＿題 時間 ＿＿＿分＿＿＿秒	答對題數 ＿＿＿題 時間 ＿＿＿分＿＿＿秒	答對題數 ＿＿＿題 時間 ＿＿＿分＿＿＿秒

35-39 題參考以下廣告與信件。

水仙花博物館會員招募
感謝您的支持

- **會員福利**
  - 免費入館，同行者一人免費（所有會員）
  - 全館消費 85 折（家庭與贊助會員）
  - 每季寄發《風之時代》雜誌（附《水仙會訊》）（個人、家庭與贊助會員）
  - 獲邀並免費參加本館的特別活動（僅限贊助會員）

- **會員費的用途**

所有會費將投入博物館作為一般基金。做為非營利機構，本館多數收入來自於捐贈。然而，為了彌補營業成本，因此需要透過入館費、商品銷售與會員費來募集資金。

- **會員年費**

本館有 4 種會員等級：

$20　學生／年長會員

$30　個人會員

$50　家庭會員

$250　贊助會員

如果您成為贊助會員，或是捐贈大筆捐款，同時也是美國納稅人的話，可申請稅額減免（進一步資訊，請聯絡博物館）。

- **支付會費**

您可透過支票或銀行匯票支付，請寄到：

水仙花博物館之友

轉交 Martin J. Druthers 博士

72800 美國德州奧斯汀查爾斯頓街 1206 號

水仙花博物館董事會

轉交 Martin J. Druthers 博士

72800 美國德州奧斯汀查爾斯頓街 1206 號

親愛的 Druthers 博士與水仙花博物館董事會：

我跟妻子於 1 月 12 日週三回國，收到來自水仙花博物館的來信，很遺憾得知，我們以一人 100 美元受邀參加水仙花博物館舞會。

這 4 年來，我們夫婦每年都各自支付 250 美元給博物館，往年從沒被收取過這筆費用。然而，更令我們驚訝的是，也無隻字片語說明今年舞會要收費的原因。我可以肯定，我那從創館以來一直捐贈大筆款項給貴館的過世祖父，要是知道這件事，也會相當失望。

此外，我們已經有超過半年時間沒有收到《風之時代》。而我最近一次與兩位好友前去貴館時，在售票處花了 10 分鐘等待確認會員編號，這令我們相當尷尬。

博物館須負起身為社區一份子的責任。想宣傳活動卻不遵守活動是相當不負責任的。我希望能收到貴館的道歉信，並且說明我們需要支付舞會費用的原因。

Taylor White 謹啟

35. 這封信的目的為何？

(A) 要求打折

(B) 取消會員

(C) 拒絕捐贈

(D) 投訴

正確答案：D　　　　　　　　　　　　　　　　文章目的

題目詢問信件目的。寄件人在信裡中提到參加舞會被收取費用、館方沒有任何說明，以及沒有收到通訊報等不滿事項，最後要求館方寫信道歉。由此可知，信的目的是為了抱怨，答案為 (D)。

36. Taylor White 擁有何種會員等級？

(A) 學生／年長會員

(B) 個人會員

(C) 家族會員

(D) 贊助會員

正確答案：D

從信件第二段第 1 行的 We have both paid $250 annually 可得知 Taylor 夫婦兩人都支付了 250 美元。此外，廣告的年會費項目裡有寫到 $250 Patron，可知一年付 250 美元的 Taylor 的會員身分是 Patron「贊助會員」。

ⓘ這題要結合兩篇文章的資訊來解題，數字是解題線索。

37. 博物館漏寄了幾本雜誌給 Taylor White？

(A) 1 本 (B) 2 本

(C) 3 本 (D) 4 本

正確答案：B

信件第三段 1 行提到 we have not received Times of the Winds for over half a year.。此外，廣告的 What do members receive? 的第 3 項也寫到 Times of the Winds magazine (with the Daffodil Newsletter) sent each quarter。由此可推論，每季推出的雜誌有半年沒收到的話，表示有兩期的雜誌漏寄了。

ⓘ這題也是要結合兩篇文章的資訊來解題。

38. 信件中第二段第 5 行的 absence 一字，意思最接近

(A) abstract「摘要」

(B) detail「細節」

(C) lack「缺少」

(D) presence「存在」

正確答案：C

信件第二段第 5 行的 absence 出現在 However, what surprised us more was the absence of an explanation 這個句子裡。absence of an explanation 是「沒有說明」的意思，與 (C) lack 同義。

39. 關於 Taylor White，信中沒有提及什麼？

(A) 他去年免費受邀參加年度舞會。

(B) 他最近一次拜訪博物館被延誤服務。

(C) 他加入會員已經有 4 年時間。

(D) 他的祖父也對差勁的對待感到失望。

正確答案：D NOT 題

信件第二段 7 行提到 I am certain that my late grandfather, who donated large sums to the museum after its founding, would be disappointed as well.。 從 my late grandfather 可得知他的祖父已不在人世，late 在此指「已逝的」。因此 (D) He has a grandfather who is also disappointed with the poor treatment. 文意不符。

ⓘ 信裡寫的 would be disappointed 是假設語氣，暗示「如果還活著的話」，在敘述與現實情況相反的事情時，會用到這個句型。

單字

- daffodil *(n.)* 水仙花
- membership *(n.)* 會員資格
- accompany *(v.)* 陪伴
- quarter *(n.)* 季度
- general fund 一般基金
- not-for-profit organization 非營利組織
- donation *(n.)* 捐款，捐獻
  (v.) donate 捐款，捐獻
- raise *(v.)* 募集（資金）
- as follows 如下
- senior citizen 年長者
- patron *(n.)* 贊助者
- taxpayer *(n.)* 納稅人
- claim *(v.)* 索求
- tax benefit 所得稅優惠
- via *(prep.)* 透過
- check *(n.)* 支票
- money order 銀行匯票

- board of trustees 董事會
- ball *(n.)* 舞會
- per plate 一人份（料理）
- regularly *(adv.)* 定期地
- charge *(v.)* 索價
- late *(adj.)* 已逝的
- sum *(n.)* 總金額
- founding *(n.)* 創立
- embarrassingly *(adv.)* 令人難堪地
- verify *(v.)* 確認
- follow through 進行到底
- irresponsible *(adj.)* 不負責任的
- including *(prep.)* 包含
- reject *(v.)* 拒絕
- neglect *(v.)* 忽略
- abstract *(n.)* 摘要
- presence *(n.)* 存在

https://www.iowatraveler.com/october-festivals-events/#post-242

Fairley Harvest Festival: Get ready for Fairley's annual autumn celebration that's fun for the whole family.

See more than 120 vegetable and flower exhibits. Or take part in a contest for your chance to win a prize! There will be food and crafts on sale as well as numerous educational sessions on topics ranging from farm animals to agricultural machinery.

Admission to the festival is $5.00 per person. Kids 12 and under are admitted free of charge with a ticketed adult. The fee to join a festival contest is $3.00.

❏ When: October 7 and 8 (9:00 A.M. to 4:30 P.M.)
❏ Where: Fairley County Fairgrounds at 94
    Cardington Road
❏ Web site: www.fairleyfestival.org
❏ Organizers: 555-4481

BACK

```
╔══════════════════════════════════════════╗
║ ≡≡≡≡≡≡≡≡≡≡ E-Mail Message ≡≡≡≡≡≡≡≡≡≡ ║
╚══════════════════════════════════════════╝
```

To: Derrick Thomson
From: Patricia Spenser
Date: October 2
Subject: Festival Entries

Dear Mr. Thomson:

Thank you for contacting us about the canned food contest.

In response to your question, all entries must be received at the contest pavilion on the festival grounds no later than noon on October 7. A panel of judges will award first, second, and third place ribbons to the tastiest entries at around 2:00 P.M. on the second day of the festival.

It is important to also be aware that entries have to be labeled with the following information: type of item, date canned, and method of processing. Please do not write your own name on the label.

For additional details on this contest, be sure to check out the "Activities" page of the festival Web site (www. fairleyfestival.org).

Warmest regards,
Patricia Spenser
Fairley Harvest Festival Organizer

Harvest Festival Contest
Spotlights Fairley's Best Can Again

Fairley County (October 14)—Anyone who has tried Claudia Ross's beef stew will not be surprised to hear that she won the canned food contest at this year's Fairley Harvest Festival. It's delicious! What may come as a surprise, though, is that her canned stew has placed first in the contest for three consecutive years.

Owner of the Roadhouse Diner on Abner Road, Claudia Ross cooks stew almost every day for her customers. But she only ever uses her canning machine for the contest.

As for the winners of the second and third place ribbons, Derrick Thomson's creamy broccoli soup and Nancy Mendez's corned beef received the accolades, respectively. All three contestants were given a certificate and a 12-, 8-, or 5-piece cookware set.

---

40. What is NOT mentioned about the event on the Web page?
    (A) It is held every year in the autumn.
    (B) It features several musical performances.
    (C) It includes opportunities to learn about animals.
    (D) It is free for some people to attend.

41. Why did Ms. Spenser write the e-mail to Mr. Thomson?

    (A) To announce a change of plans

    (B) To encourage him to volunteer

    (C) To clarify some contest rules

    (D) To propose using a new product

42. What is indicated about Mr. Thomson?

    (A) He paid $3.00 to join a contest.

    (B) He won a 5-piece cookware set.

    (C) His children are younger than 12 years old.

    (D) His specialty is beef stew.

43. Whose canned food placed third in the contest?

    (A) Patricia Spenser

    (B) Claudia Ross

    (C) Derrick Thomson

    (D) Nancy Mendez

44. What is suggested about the creamy broccoli soup?

    (A) It was made at the Roadhouse Diner.

    (B) It received an award on October 8.

    (C) It is sold in Fairley County supermarkets.

    (D) It was canned at 94 Cardington Road.

做完之後，在下方表格填入作答時間與答對題數。

第 1 回 ＿＿＿月＿＿＿日	第 2 回 ＿＿＿月＿＿＿日	第 3 回 ＿＿＿月＿＿＿日
答對題數 ＿＿＿題 時間 ＿＿＿分＿＿＿秒	答對題數 ＿＿＿題 時間 ＿＿＿分＿＿＿秒	答對題數 ＿＿＿題 時間 ＿＿＿分＿＿＿秒

翻譯及解析

40-44 題參考以下網頁，電子郵件與報導。

費爾利秋收節：全家同樂，來參加一年一度的費爾利秋天慶典。

來看看超過 120 個蔬果花卉擺攤，也可以參加比賽拿大獎！這裡會販售食物與手工藝品，也提供從農場動物到農業機器等各種具教育意義的課程活動。

入場費每人 5 元，12 歲以下的孩童有一名持票大人陪同，即可免費入場。報名比賽需收費 3 元。

❏ 時間：10 月 7 日、8 日（早上 9 點到下午 4 點半）
❏ 地點：費爾利郡露天遊樂場，查丁頓路 94 號
❏ 活動網站：www.fairleyfestival.org
❏ 主辦單位聯絡電話：555-4481

收件人：Derrick Thomson
寄件人：Patricia Spenser
日期：10 月 2 日
主旨：活動參賽產品

親愛的 Thomson 先生：

謝謝您聯絡我罐頭食物競賽一事。

在此回應您的問題。所有參賽產品都必須在 10 月 7 日中午之前，送達活動會場的比賽特設會場。活動第二天下午 2 點左右，評審團將頒發最美味參賽產品前三名勳帶。

還有一點很重要，參賽產品必須標明以下資訊：品項類別、封罐日期以及加工方式。請勿標示自家名字。

關於這項比賽的其他細節，請務必上活動官網（www. fairleyfestival.org）的「活動區」確認。

Patricia Spenser
費爾利秋收節主辦人

費爾利郡（10 月 14 日）── 每個吃過 Claudia Ross 燉牛肉的人，聽到這項產品再次獲得今年費爾利秋收節最佳罐頭的消息，應該一點都不驚訝。非常美味！不過，另一個消息應該就會讓你驚訝：這項燉牛肉罐頭已經連續 3 年在這項節慶中拿到第一。

位於 Abner 路上的 Roadhouse 餐廳老闆 Claudia Ross，幾乎天天為上門顧客燉煮燉牛肉。只有在比賽時，她才會使用罐頭機器，把燉牛肉做成罐頭。

第二名與第三名得主，則是分別由 Derrick Thomson 的花椰菜奶油濃湯與 Nancy Mendez 的鹹牛肉獲得。這 3 名參賽者將會獲得證書，並分別獲贈 12 件、8 件與 5 件廚具組。

40. 關於活動，何者沒有在網站上提及？

(A) 每年秋天舉行。　　　　　　　(B) 主打好幾組音樂表演。
(C) 有學習動物知識的機會。　　　(D) 某些人可以免費入場。

正確答案：B　　　　　　　　　　　　　　　　NOT 題

選項 (A) 對應網頁第一段 1 行的 Fairley's annual autumn celebration；(C) 對應第二段 4 行 的 numerous educational sessions on topics ranging from farm animals to agricultural machinery；(D) 則對應第三段 1 行的 Kids 12 and under are admitted free of charge with a ticketed adult. 只有 (B) 沒有與之相符的敘述。

① 多益改制後，新增的「3 篇閱讀」需閱讀 3 篇文章來解題，每次測驗會出 3 組，每組 5 題，共 15 題。

41. Spenser 小姐為什麼寫信給 Thomason 先生？

(A) 宣布計畫更動。　　　　　　　(B) 鼓勵他義務幫忙。
(C) 釐清比賽規則。　　　　　　　(D) 提出使用新產品建議。

正確答案：C　　　　　　　　　　　　　　　　文章目的

題目關鍵字是人名與 Why，對照後可知，題目要問的是電子郵件的目的。Ms. Spenser 回答 Mr. Thomson 的問題，說明參賽產品寄送地點、日期、評審資訊、與標示注意事項。因此這封電子郵件的目的是 (C) To clarify some contest rules.

42. 關於 Thomason 先生，以下何者有提及？

(A) 他付了 3 美元參加比賽。

(B) 他贏得 5 件式廚具組。

(C) 他的孩子不滿 12 歲。

(D) 他的專業是燉牛肉。

正確答案：A 　　　　　　　　　　　　　　　　　**整合資訊**

將第 3 篇報導第三段 1 行的 As for the winners of the second and third place ribbons, Derrick Thomson's creamy broccoli soup and Nancy Mendez's corned beef received the accolades, respectively.，與網頁第三段 3 行的 The fee to join a festival contest is $3.00. 結合之後即可推論出答案。榮獲第二名表示有參加比賽，而參加比賽會被索取 3 美元的報名費，答案是 (A)。

ⓘ 第 3 篇報導提到這個人在比賽榮獲了第二名。第 1 篇文章則寫到比賽的報名費是 3 美元。也就是說，這個人付了 3 美元的報名費。這篇需結合第 1 篇與第 3 篇文章的資訊來解題。

---

43. 誰的罐頭食品獲得第三名？

(A) Patricia Spenser

(B) Claudia Ross

(C) Derrick Thomson

(D) Nancy Mendez

正確答案：D 　　　　　　　　　　　　　　　　　**詢問細節**

題目的 third place「第三名」是解題關鍵字。有提及名次的是第 3 篇報導，第三段 1 行提到 As for the winners of the second and third place ribbons, Derrick Thomson's creamy broccoli soup and Nancy Mendez's corned beef received the accolades, respectively. 可知 Derrick Thomson 榮獲第二名，Nancy Mendez 是第三名。因此答案是 (D)。

ⓘ respectively 指「分別、各自」，看到這個字，就要仔細對照前後資訊。如 Tex and Masaya, 16 and 18, respectively 這個句子，意思就是 Tex 16 歲，Masaya 18 歲。

44. 關於花椰菜奶油濃湯，文中暗示了什麼？

(A) 由 Roadhouse 餐廳製作。

(B) 在 10 月 8 日得獎。

(C) 在費爾利郡的超市有販賣。

(D) 在 Cardington 路 94 號製成罐頭。

| 正確答案：B | 整合資訊 |

從報導第三段 1 行可得知，花椰菜濃湯是第二名。接著，從電子郵件第二段 3 行的 A panel of judges will award first, second, and third place ribbons to the tastiest entries at around 2:00 P.M. on the second day of the festival. 可知秋收節第二天會宣布獲獎產品。此外，網頁上寫 When: October 7 and 8 可知，秋收節第二天是 10 月 8 日。綜合以上資訊，可推論花椰菜濃湯是在 10 月 8 日獲選為第二名，答案是 (B)。

① 這種需要結合 3 篇文章資訊來解題的「3 篇文章關聯題」的出題機率不高。

單字

- harvest *(n.)/(v.)* 收成
- exhibit *(n.)/(v.)* 展示，展出
- take part in 參加 = participate in
- prize *(n.)* 獎金
- range from A to B 範圍涵蓋從 A 到 B
- farm animal 家畜
- admit *(v.)* 允許入場
- ticketed *(adj.)* 持有票券的
- fairgrounds *(n.)* 露天活動場
- organizer *(n.)* 主辦者，主辦單位
- entry *(n.)* 參賽作品
- in response to 作為～的回應
- pavilion *(n.)* 臨時會場
- no later than 在～之前

- panel of judges 評審團
- ribbon *(n.)* 緞帶
- award *(v.)/(n.)* 頒發；獎項
- be aware that 留意
- label *(v.)* 貼上標籤
- process *(v.)* 加工
- spotlight *(v.)* 引起矚目
- stew *(n.)* 燉肉
- consecutive *(adj.)* 連續的，無間斷的
- accolade *(n.)* 獎賞
- respectively *(adv.)* 分別地
- contestant *(n.)* 參賽者
- cookware *(n.)* 廚房用具
- specialty *(n.)* 專長

Questions 45-49 refer to the following Web page, comment form, and e-mail. ⊙ 35

http://www.tranzek.com/tickets/

Tranzek Buses

| HOME | SCHEDULES | STATIONS | TICKETS | NEWS | ABOUT US |

Four Easy Ways to Get Tickets...

Option 1: By filling out the reservation form **here** and then printing your ticket from your e-mail

Option 2: By using an Automated Ticket Kiosk, found at all Tranzek Bus stations

Option 3: By purchasing directly from a ticket agent at select bus stations on this **list**

Option 4: By calling us at 1-800-357-2493

Multi-Trip Tickets

For passengers who travel frequently between Tranzek Bus station locations, multi-trip tickets can be purchased at a discounted fare. These special tickets are good for 12 one-way trips and remain valid for 6 months from the date of purchase. They are available only from our Automated Ticket Kiosks.

http://www.tranzek.com/feedback-form/

Today's Date	February 2
Name	Brady Thornton
E-mail	bthornton@hivemail.com

Comment

I was in Seattle for a concert yesterday and decided to catch a bus back to Tacoma afterward instead of spending the night. Up until last month, I regularly traveled by bus between Tacoma, where I live, and Seattle, where I used to work. I always bought multi-trip tickets and had one left to get back to Tacoma. When I showed it to the ticket checker outside the bus, he said it had expired. This was disappointing because I bought the tickets just a few months ago and was sure that I'd read on Tranzek's Web site they'd be good for six months. Anyway, I had to buy another ticket from the ticket agent at the station, which cost me $8.75.

SUBMIT

To: Brady Thornton
From: Tranzek Buses
Date: February 4
Subject: Feedback Response

Dear Mr. Thornton:

Thank you for taking the time to send us your feedback. From your comment, it appears there might have been some misunderstanding. As of November 1 of last year, multi-trip tickets remain valid for three months. However, multi-trip tickets purchased before November 1 are good for six months. Our Web site was updated in November to reflect this change.

We recommend that you show the ticket to a ticket agent at our Tacoma bus station and explain the situation. If it had not expired by the date you tried to use it, you may be entitled to a full refund for the ticket you bought on February 1.

Should you have any questions, please do not hesitate to contact us again.

Sincerely,

Amy Waters
Customer Service Manager
Tranzek Buses

45. Why was Mr. Thornton in Seattle on February 1?

(A) For a job
(B) For a ceremony
(C) For a performance
(D) For a competition

46. Why was Mr. Thornton disappointed?

    (A) He was unable to get a seat on a night bus.

    (B) An event did not finish according to schedule.

    (C) A hotel did not have any vacancies.

    (D) He thought that a ticket could still be used.

47. Which ticketing option listed on the Web page did Mr. Thornton use before February 1?

    (A) Option 1

    (B) Option 2

    (C) Option 3

    (D) Option 4

48. What is suggested about the Tacoma bus station?

    (A) It does not sell multi-trip tickets.

    (B) It is included in a list on a Web site.

    (C) It was built last year.

    (D) It is near an event venue.

49. According to Ms. Waters, what was changed on the Web site?

    (A) Information regarding the period of validity for certain tickets

    (B) Details about a particular method of making a purchase

    (C) The list of bus stations with an in-house ticketing agent

    (D) The number of options available for acquiring tickets

做完之後，在下方表格填入作答時間與答對題數。

第 1 回 ＿＿月＿＿日	第 2 回 ＿＿月＿＿日	第 3 回 ＿＿月＿＿日
答對題數 ＿＿＿題 時間 ＿＿＿分＿＿＿秒	答對題數 ＿＿＿題 時間 ＿＿＿分＿＿＿秒	答對題數 ＿＿＿題 時間 ＿＿＿分＿＿＿秒

45-49 題參考以下網頁、評論留言與電子郵件。

4 種簡易的購票方式：

選項 1：填寫這裡的預約單，接著去您的電子信箱將票券列印出來。

選項 2：用自動售票機購買，各個 Tranzek 客運站皆有設置。

選項 3：直接向售票人員購買，請參考設有站務人員的客運站列表。

選項 4：撥打 Multi-Trip 售票系統的服務電話 1-800-357-2493。

Multi-Trip 車票

經常使用 Tranzek 客運旅遊的乘客，可用折扣價購買 multi-trip 車票。此特殊票券可搭乘 12 趟單次車程，自購買日起半年內有效，僅限自動售票機販售。

日期：2 月 2 日

名字：Brady Thornton

E-mail：bthornton@hivemail.com

評論：

我昨天參加完在西雅圖的一場演唱會，決定不過夜，當天搭乘客運回到塔科馬。我住在塔科馬，先前在西雅圖上班，直到上個月為止，我固定搭乘客運通勤到西雅圖。我總是購買 multi-trip 車票。回到塔科馬之後，還剩下 1 次搭乘數。當時我拿出車票靠近客運外面的驗票機，它卻顯示車票已過期。這很令人失望，因為我是幾個月前才買的，而且我保證我已經看過 Tranzek 官網上的使用說明，上面說車票在半年內有效。總之，我得向售票員補買另一張車票才能上車，花了我 8.75 美元。

收件人：Brady Thornton
寄件人：Tranzek 客運
日期：2 月 4 日
主旨：意見回饋

親愛的 Thornton 先生：

感謝您花時間寄來您的意見。根據您的評論，這當中應該是有些誤解。從去年 11 月 1 日起，multi-trip 車票有效期間已經變更成 3 個月。不過 11 月 1 日之前購買的車票，仍維持 6 個月的有效期間。我們的官網也同步於 11 月更新這項改變。

我們建議您可以向塔科馬客運站的售票員出示您的車票，並向他解釋您的狀況。如果您的車票尚未過期，您有權索取您在 2 月 1 日購票的全額退費。

若您還有任何疑問，歡迎再次聯繫我們。

Amy Waters
Tranzek 客運客服經理

---

45. 為什麼 Thornton 先生 2 月 1 日人在西雅圖？

(A) 為了工作
(B) 為了典禮
(C) 為了表演
(D) 為了比賽

正確答案：**C**

詢問細節

第 1 篇文章是客運網站上的票券資訊，第 2 篇是客運乘客留言，第 3 篇則是客運公司對乘客留言的答覆。Mr. Thornton 的名字出現在評論留言中，第一行提到 I was in Seattle for a concert yesterday，可得知 Thornton 為了看演唱會去了 Seattle。演唱會可改以 performance「演出」來稱呼，因此答案是 (C)。

①作答 3 篇閱讀題時，請先抓出各個文章主旨，找到文章之間的關係，就可快速解題。

46. 為什麼 Thornton 會失望？

(A) 他搭乘夜班巴士沒位置坐。　　(B) 活動沒有準時結束。

(C) 飯店沒有空房。　　(D) 他以為車票還能使用。

正確答案：D　　　　　　　　　　　　　　　**詢問細節**

從評論留言第 8 行的 This was disappointing because I bought the tickets just a few months ago and was sure that I'd read on Tranzek's Web site they'd be good for six months. 可知乘客失望是因為原本以為有 6 個月效期的車票卻無法使用，答案是 (D)。

ⓘ 這裡的 good for six months 的 good 指是「有效的」，與 valid 同義。

---

47. Thornton 先生在 2 月 1 日前所使用的車票，是屬於網頁的何種購買方式？

(A) 選項 1　　　　　　　　　　　　(B) 選項 2

(C) 選項 3　　　　　　　　　　　　(D) 選項 4

正確答案：B　　　　　　　　　　　　　　　**整合資訊**

從評論留言第 5 行的 I always bought multi-trip tickets and had one left to get back to Tacoma. 可判斷 Mr. Thornton 經常購買 multi-trip ticket。而網站上的 Multi-Trip Tickets 欄位裡註明：They are available only from our Automated Ticket Kiosks.，可得知 multi-trip ticket 只能透過自動售票機購買。另外，網站購買方式的選項說明裡，可看出用自動售票機購買是 option 2，答案是 (B)。

ⓘ kiosk 在英文裡也可以指販賣報章雜誌、輕食飲料的小賣店，不一定開在車站裡。

---

48. 關於塔科馬公車站，文中暗示什麼？

(A) 沒有販賣 multi-trip 車票。　　(B) 在網站上的列表中有提到。

(C) 去年才蓋好。　　　　　　　　(D) 靠近某個活動會場。

正確答案：B　　　　　　　　　　　　　　　**整合資訊**

從電子郵件第二段 We recommend that you show the ticket to a ticket agent at our Tacoma bus station 可得知 Tacoma 客運站有售票員。此外，從網站資訊的 Option 3: By purchasing directly from a ticket agent at select bus stations on this list 可得知網站上有設有售票員的客運站一覽表。答案是 (B)。

ⓘ 結合「Tacoma 客運站有售票員」（第 3 篇）與「有刊登有售票員的客運站一覽表」（第 1 篇）兩項資訊，才可得出「Tacoma 客運站有在一覽表」的結論。

49. 根據 Waters 小姐，網站上的何種資訊已變更？

(A) 某車票的有效日期相關資訊

(B) 某購買方式的細節

(C) 設有售票員的客運站列表

(D) 取得車票的方法數量

正確答案：A

整合資訊

從電子郵件第一段 3 行的 As of November 1 of last year, multi-trip tickets remain valid for three months. 可得知效期已改為 3 個月。再看到同段 6 行 Our Web site was updated in November to reflect this change. ，可知網站已同步反映這項改變。答案是 (A)。

ⓘ 這題要結合第 3 篇文章的「去年 11 月 1 日以後，回數票的效期已從 6 個月改成 3 個月」與「網站為了反映這項改變已經進行了更新」兩項資訊來解題。

單字

- kiosk *(n.)* 售票機；販賣報章雜誌的小攤位
- option *(n.)* 選項
- ticket agent 售票員
- frequently *(adv.)* 頻繁地
- fare *(n.)* 車資
- one-way *(adj.)* 單程的
- remain *(v.)* 維持
- good *(adj.)* 有效的
- valid *(adj.)* 有效的
  (n.) validity 有效
- available *(adj.)* 買得到的
- instead of 而不是
- comment *(n.)/(v.)* 評論

- regularly *(adv.)* 定期地
- expire *(v.)* 到期
- appear *(v.)* 似乎
- misunderstanding *(n.)* 誤會
- reflect *(v.)* 反映
- recommend *(v.)* 推薦
- be entitled to 有權
- refund *(n.)/(v.)* 退款
- hesitate *(v.)* 猶豫
- vacancy *(n.)* 空房，空位
- make a purchase 購買
  = purchase
- acquire *(v.)* 取得，購買

June Home Improvement Workshops at Bloomsdale Value Centers

Bathroom Sink
Saturday, June 3 (1:00–3:00 P.M.)

INSTRUCTOR: Jerry Garner
PLACE: Hickory Street Value Center

Get the skills to install a new bathroom sink basin. Learn what steps to follow to replace a sink basin and how to select the tools and supplies you need for the project.

Wall and Floor Tiles
Saturday, June 10 (1:00–2:30 P.M.)

INSTRUCTOR: Amelia Shaw
PLACE: Hickory Street Value Center

Join this workshop to learn how to select, cut, and install bathroom tiles. Attendees will receive a 10% discount on any tiles they purchase at the store on June 10.

Paint and Paper
Saturday, June 17 (1:00–3:00 P.M.)

INSTRUCTOR: Felix Martins
PLACE: Highland Mall Value Center

In this workshop, find out what you need to do interior painting right. Also get lots of tips on repairing damaged drywall as well as brush and roller painting.

Basic Plumbing
Saturday, June 24 (1:00–3:30 P.M.)

INSTRUCTOR: Roberto Lopez
PLACE: Hickory Street Value Center

This hands-on workshop will teach you the basics of home plumbing so you can change a tap, replace pipes, and fix problems with toilet cisterns.

===== E-Mail Message =====

From: Lynda Olsen
To: Garrett Walsh
Date: June 11
Subject: Highland Mall Workshop

Hi Garrett,

We had a big turnout for yesterday's workshop. A few of the participants took advantage of the exclusive discount we offered them. I'm really glad you came up with the idea. We'll definitely have to introduce more special deals for our workshops in July and thereafter.

As for the next one, I'm worried that the workshop space at your location might not be big enough to comfortably fit everyone. Twenty-three customers have signed up for it to date. I bet more people will do the same before next Saturday. So, why don't we move it here? There's still plenty of time to notify them of a change of venue.

Please let me know what you think. Thanks!

Lynda Olsen
Store Manager

```
┌─────────────────────────────────────────────────────┐
│ ≡≡≡≡≡≡≡≡≡≡≡≡≡≡≡≡  E-Mail Message  ≡≡≡≡≡≡≡≡≡≡≡≡≡≡≡≡  │
├──────────────┬──────────────────────────────────────┤
│ From:        │ Garrett Walsh                         │
├──────────────┼──────────────────────────────────────┤
│ To:          │ Lynda Olsen                          │
├──────────────┼──────────────────────────────────────┤
│ Date:        │ June 12                              │
├──────────────┼──────────────────────────────────────┤
│ Subject:     │ Highland Mall Workshop              │
└──────────────┴──────────────────────────────────────┘
```

Hi Lynda,

I checked our event registration system this morning, and twenty-five people are now signed up for Saturday's workshop here. As for space, you don't have to worry about that. Early in May, we planned out the workshop during the management meeting you were absent from. We decided to hold it in the parking lot, considering how messy it will be. Hopefully, the weather will be pleasant!

See you at Wednesday's meeting.

Garrett Walsh
Store Manager

50. According to the schedule, when can workshop participants learn about replacing pipes?
  (A) On June 3
  (B) On June 10
  (C) On June 17
  (D) On June 24

51. What does Ms. Olsen indicate in her e-mail?

(A) An instructor was late for a session.

(B) A special deal is being offered all month.

(C) Her store sold some tiles on June 10.

(D) Her workshop had to be cancelled.

52. What is Ms. Olsen concerned about?

(A) A discount procedure may be confusing.

(B) A space may be too small.

(C) Some supplies may be unavailable.

(D) Some instructions may not be clear.

53. Who most likely will conduct a workshop outdoors?

(A) Jerry Garner

(B) Felix Martins

(C) Amelia Shaw

(D) Roberto Lopez

54. What is suggested about Mr. Walsh?

(A) He is a workshop instructor.

(B) He will be absent for a management meeting.

(C) He registered for an event on June 12.

(D) He works at the Highland Mall Value Center.

做完之後，在下方表格填入作答時間與答對題數。

第 1 回 ＿＿＿月＿＿＿日	第 2 回 ＿＿＿月＿＿＿日	第 3 回 ＿＿＿月＿＿＿日
答對題數 ＿＿＿題 時間 ＿＿＿分＿＿＿秒	答對題數 ＿＿＿題 時間 ＿＿＿分＿＿＿秒	答對題數 ＿＿＿題 時間 ＿＿＿分＿＿＿秒

翻譯及解析

50-54 題參考以下行程表與電子郵件。

6 月居家修繕工作坊
Bloomsdale 居家修繕連鎖

洗臉槽 6 月 3 日星期六（下午 1-3 點） 講師：Jerry Garner 地點：哈克利街分店	**壁磚與地磚** 6 月 10 日星期六（下午 1 點 -2 點半） 講師：Amelia Shaw 地點：哈克利街分店
來學習安裝洗臉槽的技巧吧。在這個工作坊裡，你可以學到更換洗臉槽的步驟，挑選到合適的工具與用品。	來參加這場工作坊，學習挑選、切割與安裝浴磚的方法。參加者可享有當天 9 折購買店內各種磁磚。
油漆與壁紙 6 月 17 日星期六（下午 1-3 點） 講師：Felix Martins 地點：Highland 購物中心分店	**基本水管修繕** 6 月 24 日星期六（下午 1 點 -3 點半） 講師：Roberto Lopez 地點：哈克利街分店
在這場工作坊裡，找到符合您需求的室內油漆吧。您也可以學會修好損壞的灰泥板，用刷子或滾筒刷油漆的訣竅。	這場實作工作坊將會教你基本居家水管修繕，你將會更換水龍頭與水管，還能修好出問題的馬桶水箱。

收件人：Lynda Olsen
寄件人：Garrett Walsh
日期：6 月 11 日
主旨：Highland 購物中心分店

Garrett 好：

昨天的工作坊報名人數相當踴躍，一些參加者也善加利用了我們所提供的獨家優惠。我很開心你能想到這個點子。接下來的 7 月與之後的工作坊，我們一定要採用更多的特價優惠。

關於下一場工作坊，我很擔心場地空間不夠讓參加者舒適進行活動。目前已經有 23 位顧客報名，我可以肯定在下週六活動開始前，會增加到像昨天一樣的報名人數。所以，我們要不要乾脆把地點改到這裡？距離工作坊還有不少時間，足夠通知他們更改地點。

請讓我知道你的想法。謝了！

Lynda Olsen
店經理

收件人：Garrett Walsh
寄件人：Lynda Olsen
地點：6 月 12 日
主旨：Highland 購物中心分店

Lynda 好：

我今天早上看了活動報名系統，目前已經有 25 個人報名週六的工作坊。關於空間一事，你無需擔心。5 月時，我們在你缺席的主管會議上有討論過這場工作坊的事。

考量到時場地會很髒亂，我們已經決定在停車場舉辦。希望到時候天氣會很好！

週三會議見。

Garrett Walsh
店經理

50. 根據行程表，參加工作坊的人何時可學到更換水管？

(A) 6 月 3 日

(B) 6 月 10 日

(C) 6 月 17 日

(D) 6 月 24 日

關鍵字是 replacing pipes「更換水管」，行程表裡的 Basic Plumbing「基本水管修繕」的工作坊內容提到 This hands-on workshop will teach you the basics of home plumbing so you can change a tap, replace pipes, and fix problems with toilet cisterns.。這場研習活動的日期訂在 6 月 24 日，答案是 (D)。

ⓘ plumbing「水管工程」和 plumber「水管工」是 TOEIC 很常出現的單字，發音分別是 plumbing [ˋplʌmɪŋ]、plumber [ˋplʌmər]，b 不發音。

---

51. Olsen 小姐在信件中指出什麼事情？

(A) 課程講者遲到。

(B) 整個月都有促銷活動。

(C) 她的店在 6 月 10 日賣出一些磁磚。

(D) 她的工作坊取消了。

第一封電子郵件的日期是 6 月 11 日，因此電子郵件裡的 yesterday's workshop 指的是 6 月 10 日的研習活動。同一封電子郵件的第一段 1 行提到 A few of the participants took advantage of the exclusive discount we offered them.，指出參加這使用了獨家優惠，而行程表 6 月 10 日的 workshop 欄位裡也註明了 Attendees will receive a 10% discount on any tiles they purchase at the store on June 10.，表示用了 9 折折扣購買磁磚，答案是 (C)。

ⓘ 這題要結合電子郵件與行程表的資訊來解題，「使用了特別優惠」＝「用了 10% 折扣購買磁磚」的邏輯關係是解題重點。

52. Olsen 小姐擔心什麼？

(A) 折扣步驟不清不楚。

(B) 空間太小。

(C) 有些日用品賣光了。

(D) 有些教學步驟不夠清楚。

第一封電子郵件的第二段 1 行提到 As for the next one, I'm worried that the workshop space at your location might not be big enough to comfortably fit everyone.，可從這段內容得知，撰寫者擔心空間可能太小，答案是 (B)。

ⓘ might not be big enough「可能不夠大」在選項中換成了 may be too small「可能太小」來形容。

---

53. 誰最有可能主持戶外工作坊？

(A) Jerry Garner

(B) Felix Martins

(C) Amelia Shaw

(D) Roberto Lopez

題目關鍵字是 outdoors「戶外」，三篇文章中只有第二封電子郵件的第一段第 6 行有提到相關訊息：We decided to hold it in the parking lot，這裡的 it 指的是 workshop，表示這場工作坊會在停車場舉辦，此電子郵件標題是 Highland Mall Workshop，對照行程表之後，在 Highland Mall Value Center 舉辦的研習活動的講師是 Felix Martins，答案是 (B)。

ⓘ 此電子郵件也有其他線索可以輔助確定是哪場工作坊，如最後一句 how messy it will be，也可以聯想到是需要實務操作的水管修繕工作坊。

54. 關於 Walsh 先生，文中暗示什麼？

(A) 他是工作坊講師。

(B) 他將會缺席主管會議。

(C) 他報名了 6 月 12 日的活動。

(D) 他在 Highland 購物中心分店工作。

正確答案：D   **整合資訊**

從第一封電子郵件的第二段內容可得知，下一場工作坊在 Mr. Walsh 工作的店面舉辦。第一封電子郵件的日期是 6 月 11 日，因此 the next one 指的就是行程表上 6 月 17 日舉辦的研習活動，對照行程表，地點是 Highland Mall Value Center，答案是 (D)。

單字

- home improvement 居家修繕
- instructor *(n.)* 講師
- sink basin 洗臉槽
- supply *(n.)* 日用品
- paint *(n.)/(v.)* 油漆
- tip *(n.)* 訣竅
- damage *(v.)/(n.)* 損害；損傷
- drywall *(n.)* 灰泥板
- plumbing *(n.)* 配管工程，水管修繕
- hands-on *(adj.)* 親自動手的，實作的
- tap *(n.)* 水龍頭
- cistern *(n.)* 水箱
- turnout *(n.)* 到場人數
- take advantage of 利用
- exclusive *(adj.)* 獨家的

- come up with 想到
- definitely *(adv.)* 當然，毫無疑問地
- introduce *(v.)* 採用，引進，介紹
- special deal 特價
- thereafter *(adv.)* 之後
- as for 至於
- fit *(v.)* 容納
- sign up 報名
- registration *(n.)* 報名，註冊
  (v.) register 報名，註冊
- considering *(prep.)* 考量到
- messy *(adj.)* 髒亂的
- hopefully *(adv.)* 但願如此；充滿希望地
- pleasant *(adj.)*（天氣）好的；喜悅的
- confusing *(adj.)* 混淆的

NOTE

Part 1

a couple of 兩、三個～	a sense of humor 幽默感	absence (n.) 缺勤
absent (adj.) 缺席的	accept (v.) 接受	acceptance (n.) 接受
according to 根據	accountant (n.) 會計人員	accounting system 記帳系統
accurate (adj.) 準確的	achievement (n.) 功績，成就	acrobatics (n.) 雜技
additional (adj.) 額外的	address (v.) 處理（問題）	admission (n.) 入場費
advantage (n.) 優點	advertise (v.) 打廣告	advertisement (n.) 廣告，縮寫成 ad
affect (v.) 影響	afterward (adv.) 之後	agreeable (adj.) 可接受的
agricultural (adj.) 農業的	agriculture (n.) 農業	aim to 以～為目標
along with 連同	alongside (prep.) 與～一起	aluminum (n.) 鋁
among (prep.) 在～之間（用於三者以上）	amount (n.) 金額	announce (v.) 宣布
announcement (n.) 通知，公告	annual (adj.) 每年的	annually (adv.) 每年
anticipate (v.) 期待	apiece (adv.) 每個	apologize (v.) 道歉

apology (n.) 道歉	apparently (adv.) 似乎，看來	appearance (n.) 外表
appetite (n.) 食慾	applicant (n.) 申請者	application (n.) 應用程式
appreciate (v.) 感激	approval (n.) 核可，通過	approve (v.) 認可，准許
architect (n.) 建築家	architecture (n.) 建築	arrange (v.) 安排
as a token of 作為～的表示	as soon as possible 越快越好	as though 似乎
as usual 照常	assistant branch manager 分公司副經理	assume (v.) 以為，猜想
at no charge 免費	at the (very) least 至少	atmosphere (n.) 氣氛
attach (v.) 附加	attend (v.) 參加，出席	attendance (n.) 出席
author (n.) 作者	available (adj.)（房子）空出來的	avenue (n.) 大道
average (adj.) 平均的	award-winning (adj.) 得獎的	banquet (n.) 宴會
based in 總部位於	basted (adj.) 抹上油脂的	battery life 電池壽命
be accustomed to + Ving/N = be used to 習慣～，適應～	be dedicated to 致力於	be dissatisfied with 對～不滿

be home to ~ ~的發源地	be intended for 打算，作為	be interested in 對~有興趣
be open to the public 開放大眾參觀	be pertinent to 關於	be related to 與~有血緣關係
be rich with 富含	be satisfied with 對~感到滿意	before long 不久之後
beforehand (adv.) 事先	bind (v.) 裝訂（過去式與過去分詞：bound）	blend of ~的混搭
blunt (adj.)（刀子）鈍的	board meeting 董事會會議	boast of 以~自豪
brief (adj.) 簡要的	broccoli (n.) 綠花椰菜	browse (v.) 瀏覽
budget (n.) 預算	buffet (n.) 自助餐	by the time 在~時間之前
capable (adj.) 有能力的	celebrated (adj.) 有名的	centennial anniversary 一百週年
certificate (n.) 證書，證照	challenging (adj.) 有挑戰性的	client (n.) 顧客
closing address 閉幕演說	colleague (n.) 同事	come by 順道拜訪
comfort (n.) 舒適	comfortable (adj.) 舒服的	commemorate (v.) 紀念；慶祝
commemoration (n.) 紀念（儀式）	commend (v.) 讚揚	commonality (n.) 共通性

communication *(n.)* 溝通	communications department 傳訊部門	community *(n.)* 社區
compelling *(adj.)* 引人注意的	competitor *(n.)* 競爭者	complain *(v.)* 抱怨
complaint *(n.)* 抱怨	complement *(v.)* 搭配，補足	completion *(n.)* 完成
comprehensive *(adj.)* 全面的	concisely *(adv.)* 簡明扼要地	conduct *(v.)* 執行
conference *(n.)* 研討會	congratulate *(v.)* 祝賀	consider *(v.)* 考量
contact *(v.)* 聯絡	contain *(v.)* 包含	container *(n.)* 貨櫃
contraband *(n.)* 違禁品，走私品	contract *(n.)* 合約	cooperation *(n.)* 合作
corporate *(adj.)* 公司企業的	costume *(n.)* 服裝	cover *(v.)* 涵蓋，包括
crowded *(adj.)* 擁擠的	curator *(n.)* （博物館，圖書館）館長	currently *(adv.)* 目前
curved *(adj.)* 曲線的	customer *(n.)* 消費者	customer satisfaction 顧客滿意度
customer service representative 客服人員	customs *(n.)* 海關（恆用複數）	daily special 本日特餐
deadline *(n.)* 截止期限	décor *(n.)* 內裝	decorate *(v.)* 裝飾

defective *(adj.)* 有瑕疵的	delay *(n.)* 延誤	deliver *(v.)* 遞送
delivery *(n.)* 遞送	demonstrate *(v.)* 示範	demonstration *(n.)* 示範，表演
despite *(prep.)* 儘管	detail *(n.)* 詳細	detailed *(adj.)* 詳細的
develop *(v.)* 發展	diagnose *(v.)* 診斷	diagnosis *(n.)* 診斷
dim *(adj.)* 暗的	dine *(v.)* 用餐	dining establishment 餐廳
disappointing *(adj.)* 令人失望的	discount voucher 折價券	discuss *(v.)* 討論
disposal of ～的丟棄物	dispose *(v.)* 清除，丟棄（＋of）	division *(n.)* 部門
dozen *(n.)* 12 個，一打	draft *(v.)/(n.)* 起草；草案，草稿	draw *(v.)* 獲取，吸引
draw energy 注入活力	due to 由於	dull *(adj.)* 無聊的
durability *(n.)* 耐用度	durable *(adj.)* 耐用的	dynamic *(adj.)* 充滿活力的
eagerly *(adv.)* 熱切地	electronics *(n.)* 電器	employ *(v.)* 雇用
employee *(n.)* 員工	employer *(n.)* 雇主	employment *(n.)* 雇用

en route / enroute *(adv.)* 途中	encourage *(v.)* 鼓勵	endeavor *(v.)* 竭盡全力
engaged *(adj.)* 已預約的；忙線中； 有人使用的	engagement *(n.)* 從事	entertainment *(n.)* 娛樂活動
environment *(n.)* 環境	equipment *(n.)* 器材，設備	establish *(v.)* 建立
established *(adj.)* 已確立的；知名的	estimate *(n.)* 估價單；評估	estimate *(v.)* 估價
etiquette *(n.)* 禮儀	even though 即使	evolve *(v.)* 進化
examine *(v.)* 分析	exceptional *(adj.)* 出色的，優異的	executive *(n.)* 主管，經理
exhibition *(n.)* 展示	expect *(v.)* 期待，預期	experience *(n.)* 經驗
expert *(n.)* 專家	explain *(v.)* 解釋	express delivery 快遞
extend *(v.)* 延長	extension *(n.)* 延長；擴建；分機	extra *(adj.)* 額外的
face *(v.)* 面對	facility *(n.)* 設施	fail *(v.)* 失敗
favor *(v.)* 偏好	feasibility *(n.)* 可行性	feature *(n.)* 特色
feature *(v.)* 以～為特色，主打	fee *(n.)* 費用	feedback *(n.)* 回饋

fiction *(n.)* 小說	figure out 想出（辦法）	fill out/in 填寫
fine *(adj.)* 高級的	first-rate *(adj.)* 一流的	fiscal year 會計年度 = financial year
flare *(n.)* 風味	flyer *(n.)* 傳單	followed by 接著是，隨後是
forecast *(n.)/(v.)* 預測，當動詞時 三態同型	former *(adj.)* 先前的	found *(v.)* 創立
foundation *(n.)* 創立	frontline *(adj.)* 前線的；直接與客戶 面對面的	gain *(v.)* 獲得
genre *(n.)* 類型，體裁	get a hold of 聯絡～	go over 仔細查看
go with 選擇，搭配～	good faith 誠意	gratuity *(n.)* 小費
grill *(n.)/(v.)* 燒烤	guarantee *(v.)* 保證	handle *(v.)* 處理
handy *(adj.)* 方便的	hardcopy *(n.)* 紙本	hardware *(n.)* 硬體
has something for everyone 能滿足每個人的	hazardous *(adj.)* 危險的	headquarters *(n.)* 總部（恆加 s，單複數 同型）
healer *(n.)* 治療者	herb *(n.)* 香草	hesitate *(v.)* 猶豫
high-profile *(adj.)* 知名的	hold up 耽擱，延誤	hot spot 人氣景點

however (adv.) 然而	human resources 人力資源	I'd rather 我更偏好～
ideal (adj.) 理想的	identify (v.) 定義；確認	immediately (adv.) 立即
impress (v.) 使～印象深刻	impression (n.) 印象	in business 營業中的
in case of 在～狀況下	in mind 記住	in particular 尤其
in progress 進行中	income (n.) 收入	incorrect (adj.) 錯誤的
increase (v.)/(n.) 增加（動詞重音在 後，名詞重音在前）	indicate (v.) 指出	individual (adj.) 個別的，個人的
individual (n.) 個人	industry (n.) 業界	inevitable (adj.) 無法避免的
infer (v.) 推論	inform (v.) 通知	inquire (v.) 詢問
inquiry (n.) 詢問	insight (n.) 洞察力	inspect (v.) 檢查
inspection (n.) 檢查	instruction booklet 說明小冊子	instructive (adj.) 具教育意義的，具啟 發性的
interaction (n.) 互動	interrupt (v.) 中斷；打擾	interruption (n.) 中斷；打擾
invaluable (adj.) 寶貴的	inventory (n.) 倉庫	invoice (n.) 發票

issue *(n.)* 問題	item *(n.)* 品項	job responsibility 職責;工作描述
julienne *(adj.)* 切絲的	keep in mind that 記住～	launch *(v.)* 啟用;動工
lead to 導致,促成～	lie *(v.)*(問題或責任)在於	located *(adj.)* 位於～的
location *(n.)* 地點	longest-running business 老字號店家	look forward to + Ving/N 期待～
look into 調查	lower *(v.)* 減低	mainly *(adv.)* 主要
maintain *(v.)* 維持	make sure 確保	malfunction *(v.)* 故障
management experience 管理經驗	manufacture *(v.)* 大量製造	market trend 市場趨勢
masterpiece *(n.)* 傑作	match *(v.)* 使相配	material *(n.)* 材料;教材
mayor *(n.)* 市長	medical *(adj.)* 醫學的	memo *(n.)* 公司內部通知,備忘錄
mention *(v.)* 提及	meticulous *(adj.)* 嚴謹的	modification *(n.)* 修正
modify *(v.)* 修正	must-read *(n.)* 必讀作品	nearly *(adv.)* 幾乎
newly opened 新開幕的	nightly *(adj.)* 每夜的	normal *(adj.)* 一般的

not A until B 直到 B 才 A	**notable** *(adj.)* 知名的	**notice** *(n.)* 公告
notify *(v.)* 告知	**novel** *(adj.)* 新式的	**occasion** *(n.)* 特殊場合或事宜
on a weekly basis 每週	**on display** 展示中	**on top of** 除了～之外，還有
once (conj.) 一旦	**opening** *(n.)* 職缺	**opportunity** *(n.)* 機會
originally *(adv.)* 原本	**out of one's hands** 不受控制的	**overall** *(adj.)* 整體的
overall *(adv.)* 整體上	**overcast** *(adj.)*（天候）多雲陰暗的	**overlook** *(v.)* 俯瞰
overseas *(adj.)* 海外的	**overseas** *(adv.)* 在海外	**oversight** *(n.)* 失察，疏忽
package *(n.)* 包裝	**packaging** *(n.)* 包裝方式	**packed** *(adj.)* 客滿的，擁擠的
parasite *(n.)* 寄生蟲	**parcel** *(n.)* 包裹	**particularly** *(adv.)* 尤其，特別
patronage *(n.)* 光顧	**pay period** 發薪週期	**paycheck** *(n.)* 薪水
payday *(n.)* 發薪日	**payroll department** 薪資部門	**payslip** *(n.)* 薪資條，薪資明細
perform *(v.)* 表演	**performance** *(n.)* 演奏	**permanent position** 正式職缺

personnel *(n.)* 人事；員工	pick-up *(n.)* 領取（某物）；接送（某人）	place an order 下訂單，購買
pleased *(adj.)* 感到喜悅的	policy *(n.)* 政策	portfolio *(n.)* 攝影集；作品集
portrait *(n.)* 肖像	position *(n.)* 職位	post *(n.)/(v.)* 職缺；委派，派駐
preferred *(adj.)* 更好的，更合意的	pre-registration *(n.)* 事前報名	previous *(adj.)* 先前的
prior *(adj.)* 先前的	product specifications 產品規格	professional *(adj.)* 職業的；專業的
proficiency *(n.)* 精通	profile *(n.)* 簡介	profound *(adj.)* 強烈的；深刻的
project *(n.)* 提案，專案	projector *(n.)* 投影機	promote *(v.)* 宣傳，促銷；升職
promotion *(n.)* 促銷	promptly *(adv.)* 迅速地	property *(n.)* 房產，物件
proposal *(n.)* 提案	propose *(v.)* 提出	publicize *(v.)* 公布；宣傳
purchase *(n.)/(v.)* 購買（物）；購買	purchase request form 採購單	purpose *(n.)* 目的
pursue *(v.)* 追求	quantity *(n.)* 數量	question *(v.)/(n.)* 疑問，質疑；問題
rare *(adj.)* 稀少的	rate *(n.)* 價格	reach *(v.)* 到達

reader-friendly *(adj.)* 易讀的	real estate 不動產	reasonable *(adj.)* 價格合理的
recently *(adv.)* 最近	recipient *(n.)* 收件者	recommend *(v.)* 推薦
recommendation *(n.)* 推薦	recruit *(v.)* 招募	recruitment *(n.)* 招募
rectangular *(adj.)* 長方形的	recycle *(v.)* 回收利用	redesign *(n.)* 設計變更
reference *(n.)* 推薦信	refund *(v.)/(n.)* 退款	regarding *(prep.)* 關於
regardless *(adv.)* 儘管如此	region *(n.)* 區域	regulation *(n.)* 規定
relationship *(n.)*（人際）關係	release *(n.)* 上市，推出	relevant *(adj.)* 相關的
relocate *(v.)* 搬遷，搬家	remind *(v.)* 提醒	renewal *(n.)* 更新，翻新
renovate *(v.)* 翻修	renovation *(n.)* 改裝，翻修	rent *(v.)/(n.)* 租借；租金
reputation *(n.)* 名譽	request *(v.)* 請求	require *(v.)* 要求，規定
requirement *(n.)* 必備條件	research *(n.)* 研究	reservation *(n.)* 預約
reserve *(v.)* 預約	residence *(n.)* 住所，居住地	resident *(n.)* 居民

reside (v.) 居住	resistance (n.) 抵抗力	respect (v.)/(n.) 尊敬
respond (v.) 回應	responsible (adj.) 有責任的，負責～的	rest of 其餘的～
résumé (n.) 履歷	retail store 零售店	retailer (n.) 零售商
review (n.)/(v.) 審查；評論	reviewer (n.) 評論者	run (v.) 營運；運轉；進行
sales figure 銷售數字	sales representative 銷售員	sample (v.)/(n.) 試吃；試吃品， 試用品
scientific (adj.) 科學的	score high 獲得高分	sculptor (n.) 雕塑家
sculpture (n.) 雕塑品	security (n.) 保全人員	security camera 監視攝影機
self-help (adj.) 自我提升的	serve (v.) 供應（餐點）， 提供（服務）	settle on 決定
several (adj.) 數個的	severe weather 惡劣天候	shipping charge 運費
shrimp (n.) 蝦	sign (v.) 簽名	signature (n.) 簽名
signature dessert 招牌甜點	sincerely (adv.) 真誠地	sloped (adj.) 斜的
solicit (v.) 請求	specialist (n.) 專家	specifically (adv.) 特地，專門地

spice *(n.)* 調味料	spouse *(n.)* 配偶	staff *(n.)* 全體員工（集合名詞，需與複數動詞連用）
stained *(adj.)* 弄髒的	starter *(n.)* 前菜	state *(v.)* 敘述
status *(n.)* 狀況	stay *(v.)* 維持某種狀態（＋ adj.）	steady *(adj.)* 穩定的
store *(v.)* 儲存	strategy *(n.)* 策略	strengthen *(v.)* 加強
strive to 努力～	stroll *(v.)* 散步	studio *(n.)*（攝影室或錄音室等）工作室
stuffed *(adj.)* 塞滿的	subject *(n.)* 主旨	submit *(v.)* 提交，繳交
subordinate *(n.)* 下屬	successful candidate 錄取者	successor *(n.)* 繼任者
suffice *(v.)* 足夠	summary *(n.)* 概要，大綱	superior *(adj.)/(n.)* 優於的；上司
supplier *(n.)* 供應商	supplies *(n.)* 供給品（常用複數）	surveillance *(n.)* 監視
survey *(n.)/(v.)* 調查	swordfish *(n.)* 劍魚	take place 舉行
technician *(n.)* 技術人員	template *(n.)* 範本	terrace *(n.)* 露天座位區，露天平台
the present 現在	thorough *(adj.)* 仔細徹底的	thoroughly *(adv.)* 徹底地

ticket collector 收票員	toast *(v.)/(n.)* 舉杯祝賀；慶祝會	tortilla *(n.)* 墨西哥薄餅
trace *(v.)* 追溯，查出	trainee *(n.)* 受訓者	trainer *(n.)* 訓練者
transfer *(v.)/(n.)* 轉移；調動	travel *(v.)/(n.)* 出差；旅遊	treatment *(n.)* 對待，待遇；治療
tribal *(adj.)* 部落的	tribe *(n.)* 部落	turn off 關閉電源 = switch off
unavailable *(adj.)* 無法取得的；沒空的	unbeatable *(adj.)* 無法超越的	undergo *(v.)* 歷經
unexpected *(adj.)* 出乎意料的	uninteresting *(adj.)* 無趣的	unveil *(v.)* 公開，揭開
upcoming *(adj.)* 即將舉行的	upholstery *(n.)* 家飾品	upload *(v.)* 上傳
up-to-date *(adj.)* 最新的	usability *(n.)* 好用，操作順手	valuable *(adj.)* 有價值的
venue *(n.)* 會場	verify *(v.)* 確認；證實	version *(n.)* 版本
volunteer *(v.)/(n.)* 自願服務；志願者	warn *(v.)* 警告	weight *(n.)* 重量
well of information 大量資訊	well-known *(adj.)* 有名的	wine seminar 品酒會
workload *(n.)* 工作量	worthless *(adj.)* 毫無價值的	wrap up 完成，總結

Part 2

22-story *(adj.)* 22 層樓高的	**a range of** 各種的	**absence** *(n.)* 缺席
absent *(adj.)* 缺席的	**abstract** *(n.)* 摘要	**accolade** *(n.)* 獎賞
accompany *(v.)* 陪伴	**accordingly** *(adv.)* 相應地；因此	**accumulate** *(v.)* 收集，累積
acquire *(v.)* 取得，購買	**admit** *(v.)* 允許入場	**adventure** *(n.)* 冒險
adventurer *(n.)* 冒險家	**affect** *(v.)* 影響	**affix** *(v.)* 使固定
airport shuttle 機場接駁巴士	**allow** *(v.)* 允許	**amber** *(adj.)/(n.)* 琥珀色的；琥珀
amenity *(n.)* 便利設施	**animated** *(adj.)* 動畫的	**annoying** *(adj.)* 惱人的
antique *(adj.)/(n.)* 古董的；古董	**appear** *(v.)* 似乎	**application** *(n.)* 申請（表）
appointment *(n.)* 會面	**approximately** *(adv.)* 大約	**armoire** *(n.)* 衣櫃
around the clock 全天運作的	**article** *(n.)* 文章，報導	**as follows** 如下
as for 至於	**assemble** *(v.)* 組裝	**assembly** *(n.)* 組裝
assistant *(n.)* 助理	**assure** *(v.)* 向（某人）保證（某事）	**audiovisual equipment** 音響視聽設備

automatically *(adv.)* 自動地	available *(adj.)* 買得到的	award *(v.)/(n.)* 頒發；獎項
award-winning *(adj.)* 獲獎的	ball *(n.)* 舞會	ballroom *(n.)* 宴會廳
be aware that 留意	be entitled to 有權	be set to 即將 = be about to
board of trustees 董事會	booth *(n.)*（展場）棚位；電話亭	botany *(n.)* 植物學
brass *(n.)* 黃銅	bring ~ to life 賦予～生命，使～變得生動	cabinet *(n.)* 櫥櫃
catering *(n.)* 外燴服務	character *(n.)* 角色	charge *(v.)* 索價
chase *(v.)* 追逐	check *(n.)* 支票	cistern *(n.)* 水箱
claim *(v.)* 索求	clockwise *(adv.)/(adj.)* 順時針	combine *(v.)* 結合
come along （人）現身，（物）出現； 跟隨	come up with 想到	commemorate *(v.)* 慶祝，紀念
comment *(n.)/(v.)* 評論	completion *(n.)* 完成	complimentary *(adj.)* 免費的
concept *(n.)* 概念	concern *(v.)* 有關係	concerned *(adj.)* 擔心的
consecutive *(adj.)* 連續的，無間斷的	consider *(v.)* 考慮	considering *(prep.)* 考量到

construction *(n.)* 建築工程	consult *(v.)* 諮詢，請教	consulting firm 顧問公司
contestant *(n.)* 參賽者	continent *(n.)* 洲	convention *(n.)* 大型會議、集會
conversation *(n.)* 會話	cookware *(n.)* 廚房用具	craft *(n.)* 手工藝
custom-made *(adj.)* 訂製的	daffodil *(n.)* 水仙花	damage *(v.)/(n.)* 損害；損傷
dawn *(n.)* 黎明	decide on 選定	definitely *(adv.)* 當然，毫無疑問地
deliver *(v.)* 寄送	depart *(v.)* 出發	designated *(adj.)* 指定的
detect *(v.)* 偵測	direct *(v.)* 導演	director *(n.)* 導演
discount *(n.)* 折扣	distinctive *(adj.)* 有特色的	district *(n.)* 地區
donate *(v.)* 捐款，捐贈	donation *(n.)* 捐款，捐贈	draw *(v.)* 吸引（注意）
dreary *(adj.)* 沈悶的	drywall *(n.)* 灰泥板	dusk *(n.)* 黃昏
elegant *(adj.)* 優雅的	embarrassingly *(adv.)* 令人難堪地	encourage *(v.)* 鼓勵
enhance *(v.)* 提升，加強	enter into 簽訂（合約）	enthusiasm *(n.)* 熱忱

enthusiast *(n.)* 愛好者	enthusiastic *(adj.)* 熱衷的	entry *(n.)* 參賽作品
exclusive *(adj.)* 獨家的	exhibit *(n.)/(v.)* 展示，展出	expire *(v.)* 到期
extension *(n.)* 分機	fairgrounds *(n.)* 露天活動場	fare *(n.)* 車資
farm animal 家畜	fast-paced *(adj.)* 步調快的	fees apply 需付費
figure out 理解	film *(n.)* 電影，影片	fit *(v.)* 容納
fitting *(n.)* 配件，附件	follow through 進行到底	founding *(n.)* 創立
frequently *(adv.)* 頻繁地	fully booked 預約已滿的	general fund 一般基金
general public 一般民眾	get off 下（大眾交通工具）	glow *(v.)* 發光
go on sale 發售	good *(adj.)* 有效的	ground stake 接地樁
guarantee *(v.)* 保證	hands-on *(adj.)* 親自動手的，實作的	harvest *(n.)/(v.)* 收成
have trouble + Ving 做～遇到困難	hesitate *(v.)* 猶豫	hit *(n.)* 大受歡迎的東西
home improvement 居家修繕	hopefully *(adv.)* 但願如此； 充滿希望地	in advance 預先

in charge of 負責～	in response to 作為～的回應	in the middle of nowhere 位於荒郊野外
including *(prep.)* 包含	initiate *(v.)* 開始	inquire *(v.)* 詢問
inquiry *(n.)* 詢問	insert *(v.)* 插入	install *(v.)* 安裝
installation *(n.)* 安裝	instead of 而不是	instruct *(v.)* 指示，指導
instructions *(n.)*（常用複數）說明書； 說明，指示	instructor *(n.)* 講師	interest *(n.)* 興趣，關注
introduce *(v.)* 採用，引進，介紹	involvement *(n.)* 參與	irresponsible *(adj.)* 不負責任的
kiosk *(n.)* 售票機；販賣報章雜誌 的小攤位	label *(v.)* 貼上標籤	landscaping *(n.)* 造景，景觀美化
late *(adj.)* 已逝的	LCD TV 液晶電視，LCD 為 liquid crystal display 縮寫	license agreement 授權合約
make a purchase 購買 = purchase	managing director 董事總經理	manufacturer *(n.)* 製造商
mark *(v.)* 做記號	matching *(adj.)* 匹配的	membership *(n.)* 會員資格
mere *(adj.)* 一點點的	merge *(v.)* 合併	messy *(adj.)* 髒亂的
microscope *(n.)* 顯微鏡	midnight *(n.)* 凌晨 12 點，午夜	misunderstanding *(n.)* 誤會

money order 銀行匯票	moreover (adv.) 再者	motivate (v.) 激勵
narrate (v.) 擔任旁白	narrator (n.) 旁白	neglect (v.) 忽略
no later than 在～之前	not-for-profit organization 非營利組織	novel (n.) 小說
offer (n.)/(v.) 提議	on a business trip 因商外出，出差	on board 在車上
on schedule 進度如期的	on the big screen （電影）上映中的	on the edge of one's seat （因興奮激動）坐立不安
on the market 上市	one-way (adj.) 單程的	operate (v.) 營業
option (n.) 選項	organizer (n.) 主辦者，主辦單位	outdoor (adj.) 戶外的
oversee (v.) 監督	overtime (adv.)/(n.) 加班	paint (n.)/(v.) 油漆
panel of judges 評審團	pass out 發放	passenger (n.) 乘客
patron (n.) 贊助者	pave (v.) 鋪設	pavilion (n.) 臨時會場
per plate 一人份（料理）	permit (v.) 允許	photocopy (v.)/(n.) 影印
place an ad 刊登廣告	plan out 籌劃	pleasant (adj.)（天氣）好的；喜悅的

plenty of 大量的	plumbing *(n.)* 配管工程，水管修繕	population *(n.)* 人口
presence *(n.)* 存在	prize *(n.)* 獎金	process *(v.)/(n.)* 加工；步驟
productive *(adj.)* 多產的	promote *(v.)* 促銷	prove *(v.)* 證明
purchase *(v.)* 購買	purchaser *(n.)* 購買人	quality *(n.)* 品質
quarter *(n.)* 季度	R&D department 研究開發部 （R&D = research and development）	race against time 與時間賽跑
raise *(v.)* 募集（資金）	range from A to B 範圍涵蓋從 A 到 B	realize *(v.)* 發現
realtor *(n.)* 房屋仲介	recall *(v.)* 回想	rechargeable *(adj.)* 可充電的
recommend *(v.)* 推薦	reflect *(v.)* 反映	refund *(n.)/(v.)* 退款
register *(v.)* 報名，註冊	registration *(n.)* 報名，註冊	regularly *(adv.)* 定期地
reject *(v.)* 拒絕	remain *(v.)* 維持	remodel *(v.)* 改建，改裝
reproduction *(n.)* 複製品	respectively *(adv.)* 分別地	reveal *(v.)* 揭開
revision *(n.)* 修訂	ribbon *(n.)* 緞帶	ribbon-cutting ceremony 剪綵儀式，啟用儀式

route *(n.)* 路線	rundown *(adj.)* 荒廢的	rural area 郊區
sales agent 經銷商	secret society 祕密組織	see the point of 理解～的重要性
senior citizen 年長者	sensor *(n.)* 感應器	serve a need 滿足需求
set up 組裝	shade *(n.)* 色調；陰影	shady *(adj.)* 可疑的
shipping *(n.)* 運送	shipping price 運費	sign up 報名
sink basin 洗臉槽	slide *(v.)* 使滑動	slot *(n.)* 溝槽
solar *(adj.)* 太陽能的	spare moment 空閒	speaker phone 免持電話
special deal 特價	specialty *(n.)* 專長	spotlight *(v.)* 引起矚目
square feet 平方英尺	staffing *(n.)* 人員配備	startup cost 創業成本
stationery *(n.)* 文具	stew *(n.)* 燉肉	streetcar *(n.)* 路面電車
sum *(n.)* 總金額	supervise *(v.)* 監督	supervision *(n.)* 監督
supervisor *(n.)* 上司	supply *(n.)* 日用品	take advantage of 利用

take care of 處理，負責	take part in 參加 = participate in	take the time + to V 花時間做～
tap (n.) 水龍頭	target (v.)/(n.) 鎖定；目標	tax benefit 所得稅優惠
taxpayer (n.) 納稅人	text (v.)/(n.) 傳訊；文字訊息	thereafter (adv.) 之後
ticket agent 售票員	ticketed (adj.) 持有票券的	tip (n.) 訣竅
trade show 貿易展	transfer (n.) 轉乘	transit authority 交通局
trap (v.)/(n.) 設陷阱捕捉（常用作被動式）；陷阱	turn in 遞送	turnout (n.) 到場人數
TV series 連續劇	unfold (v.)（故事）展開	user manual 使用手冊
vacancy (n.) 空房，空位	valid (adj.) 有效的	validity (n.) 有效
venue (n.) 會場	verify (v.) 確認	via (prep.) 透過
villain (n.) 反派	worth (adj.) 價值～的	

EZ TALK

New TOEIC 新制多益閱讀搶分寶典
1 駅 1 題！TOEIC L&R TEST 読解特急

作　　者：神崎正哉、TEX 加藤、Daniel Warriner	
譯　　者：劉建池	
審　　訂：蕭志億	
編　　輯：鄭莉璇	
修潤校對：鄭莉璇	
封面設計：管仕豪	
內頁排版：張靜怡	
行銷企劃：陳品萱	

發 行 人：洪祺祥
副總經理：洪偉傑
副總編輯：曹仲堯
法律顧問：建大法律事務所
財務顧問：高威會計事務所

出　　版：日月文化出版股份有限公司
製　　作：EZ 叢書館
地　　址：臺北市信義路三段 151 號 8 樓
電　　話：(02) 2708-5509
傳　　真：(02) 2708-6157
網　　址：www.heliopolis.com.tw
郵撥帳號：19716071 日月文化出版股份有限公司

總 經 銷：聯合發行股份有限公司
電　　話：(02) 2917-8022
傳　　真：(02) 2915-7212
印　　刷：中原造像股份有限公司
初　　版：2020 年 6 月
定　　價：380 元
I S B N：978-986-248-888-1

New TOEIC 新制多益閱讀搶分寶典／神崎正哉，TEX 加藤，Daniel Warriner 著；劉建池譯.
-- 初版 . -- 臺北市：日月文化，2020.06
256 面；16.7×23 公分（EZ Talk）
譯自：1 駅 1 題 !TOEIC L&R TEST 読解特急
ISBN 978-986-248-888-1（平裝）

1. 多益測驗

805.1895　　　　　　　　　　　109006634